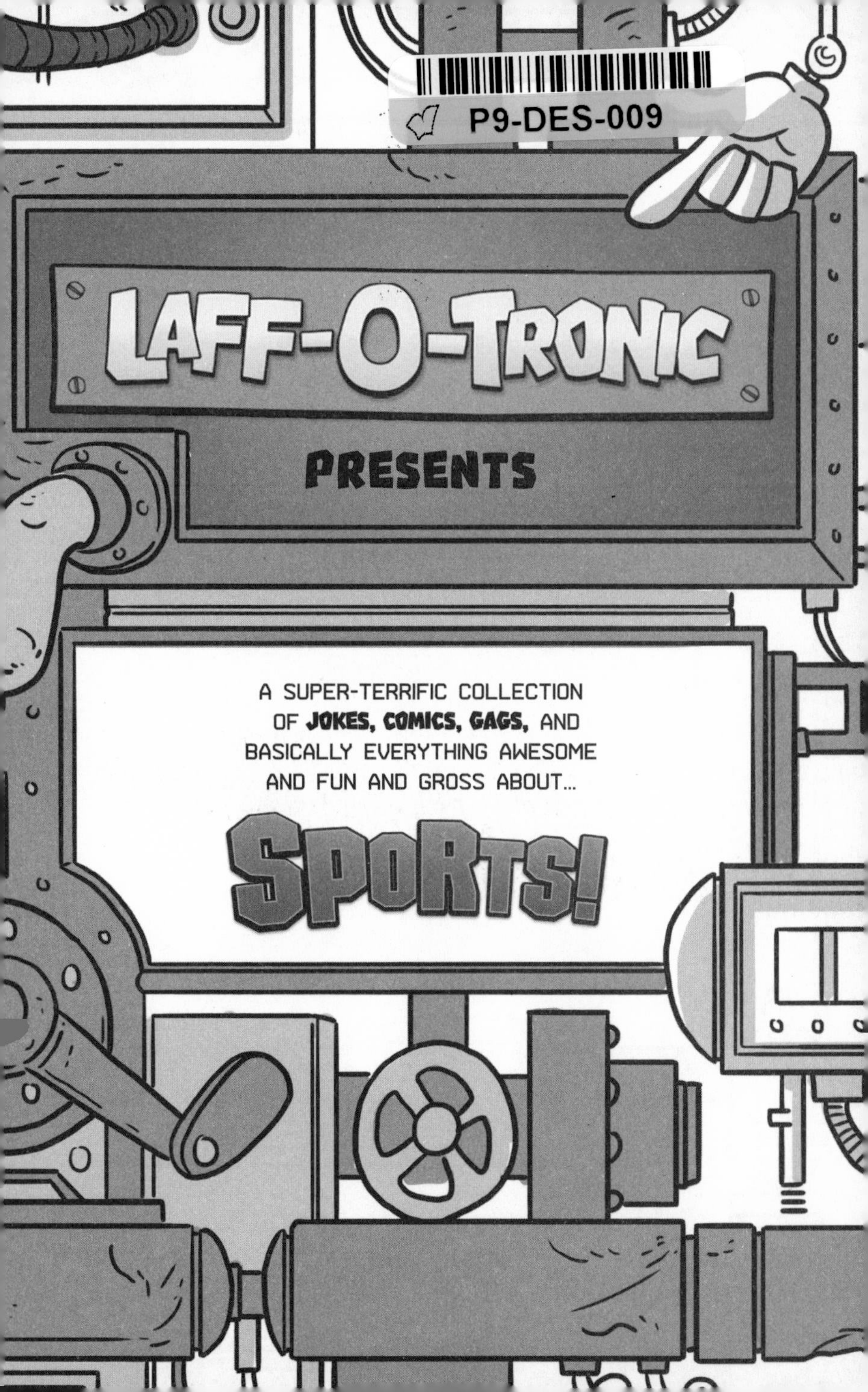
LAFF-O-TRONIC
PRESENTS
A SUPER-TERRIFIC COLLECTION OF JOKES, COMICS, GAGS, AND BASICALLY EVERYTHING AWESOME AND FUN AND GROSS ABOUT...
SPORTS!

BORING STUFF...

LAFF-O-TRONIC JOKE BOOKS! IS PUBLISHED
BY STONE ARCH BOOKS, A CAPSTONE IMPRINT
1710 ROE CREST DRIVE
NORTH MANKATO, MN 56003
WWW.CAPSTONEYOUNGREADERS.COM

CATALOGING-IN-PUBLICATION DATA IS AVAILABLE
ON THE LIBRARY OF CONGRESS WEBSITE.
ISBN: 978-1-4342-6023-9 (LIBRARY HARDCOVER)
ISBN: 978-1-4342-6193-9 (PAPERBACK)

DESIGNER: RUSSELL GRIESMER
EDITOR: DONALD LEMKE

PRINTED IN THE UNITED STATES OF AMERICA
IN STEVENS POINT, WISCONSIN.
012014   007985R

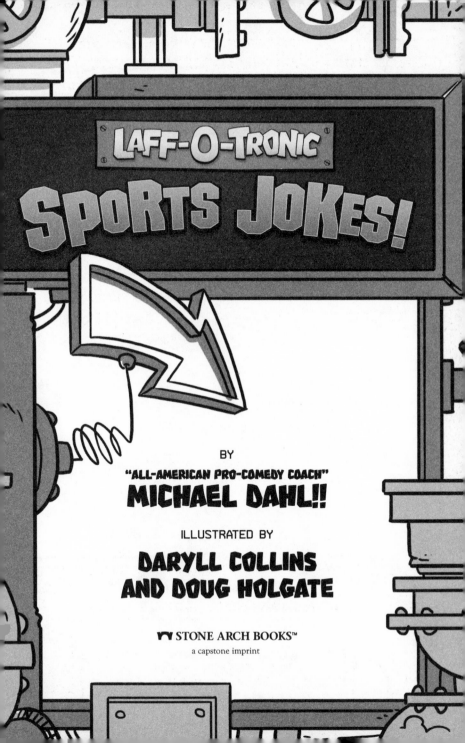

LAFF-O-TRONIC
SPORTS JOKES!

BY
"ALL-AMERICAN PRO-COMEDY COACH"
MICHAEL DAHL!!

ILLUSTRATED BY

DARYLL COLLINS
AND DOUG HOLGATE

STONE ARCH BOOKS™
a capstone imprint

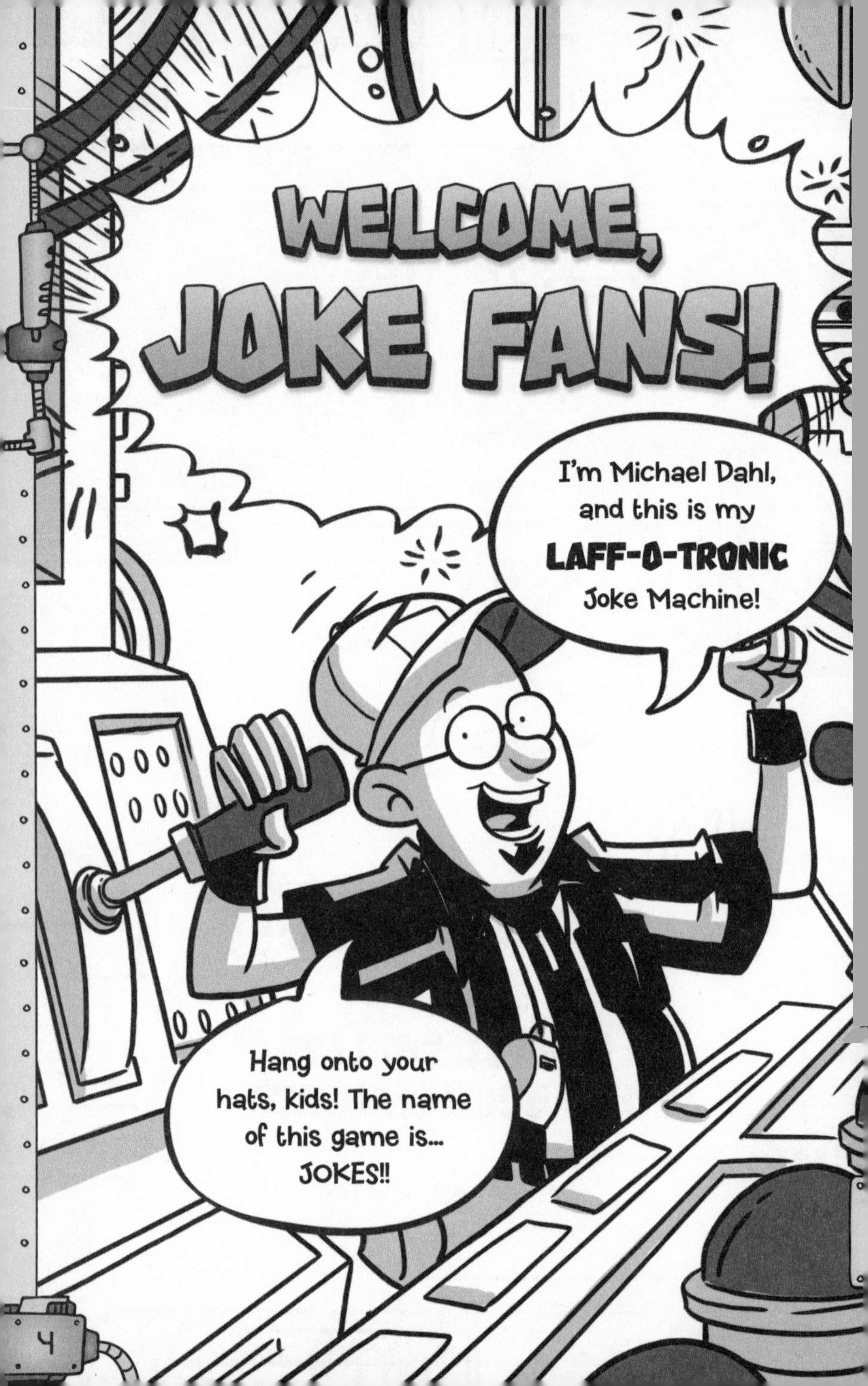
WELCOME, JOKE FANS!
I'm Michael Dahl, and this is my LAFF-O-TRONIC Joke Machine!
Hang onto your hats, kids! The name of this game is... JOKES!!

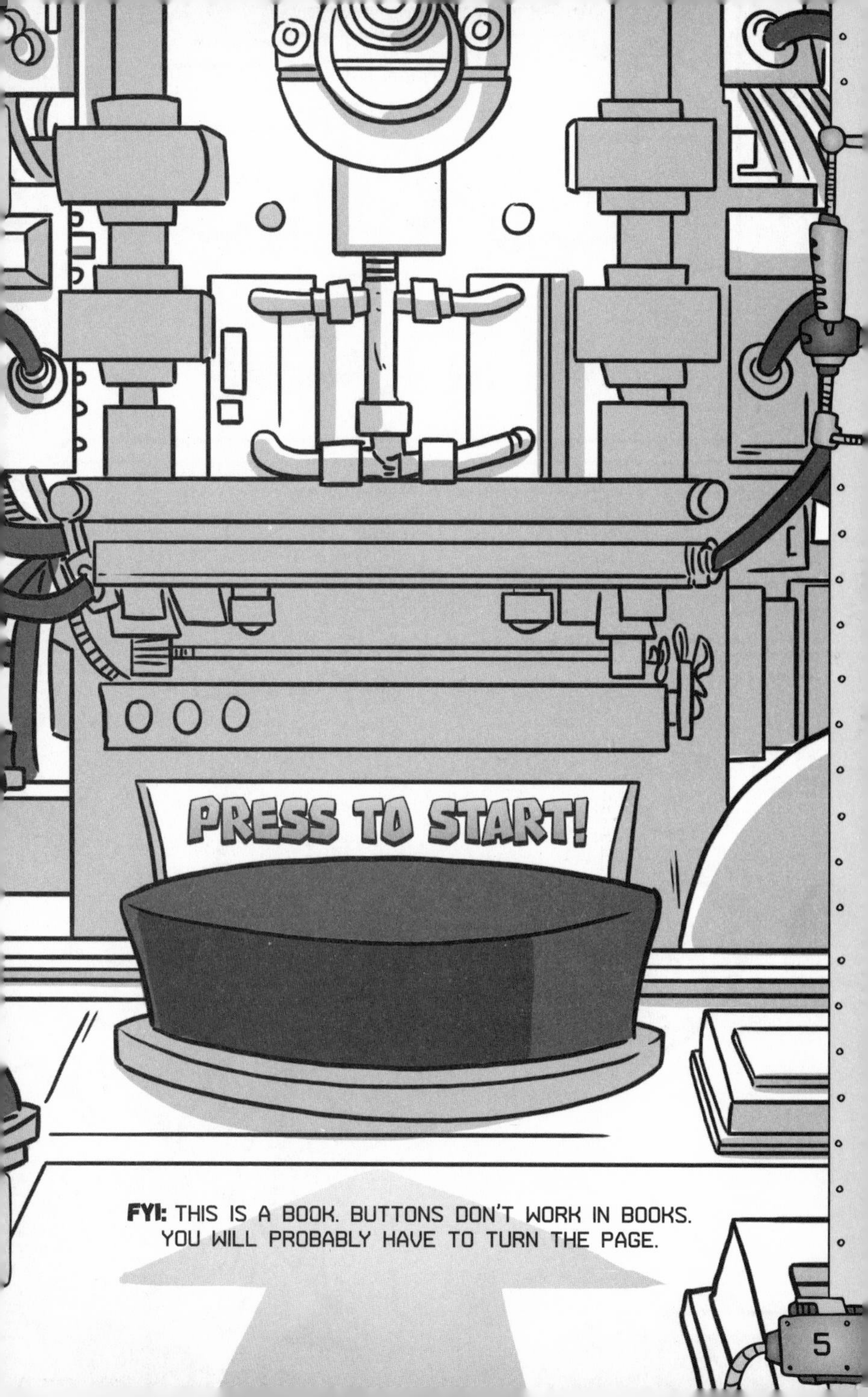
PRESS TO START!
FYI: THIS IS A BOOK. BUTTONS DON'T WORK IN BOOKS. YOU WILL PROBABLY HAVE TO TURN THE PAGE.

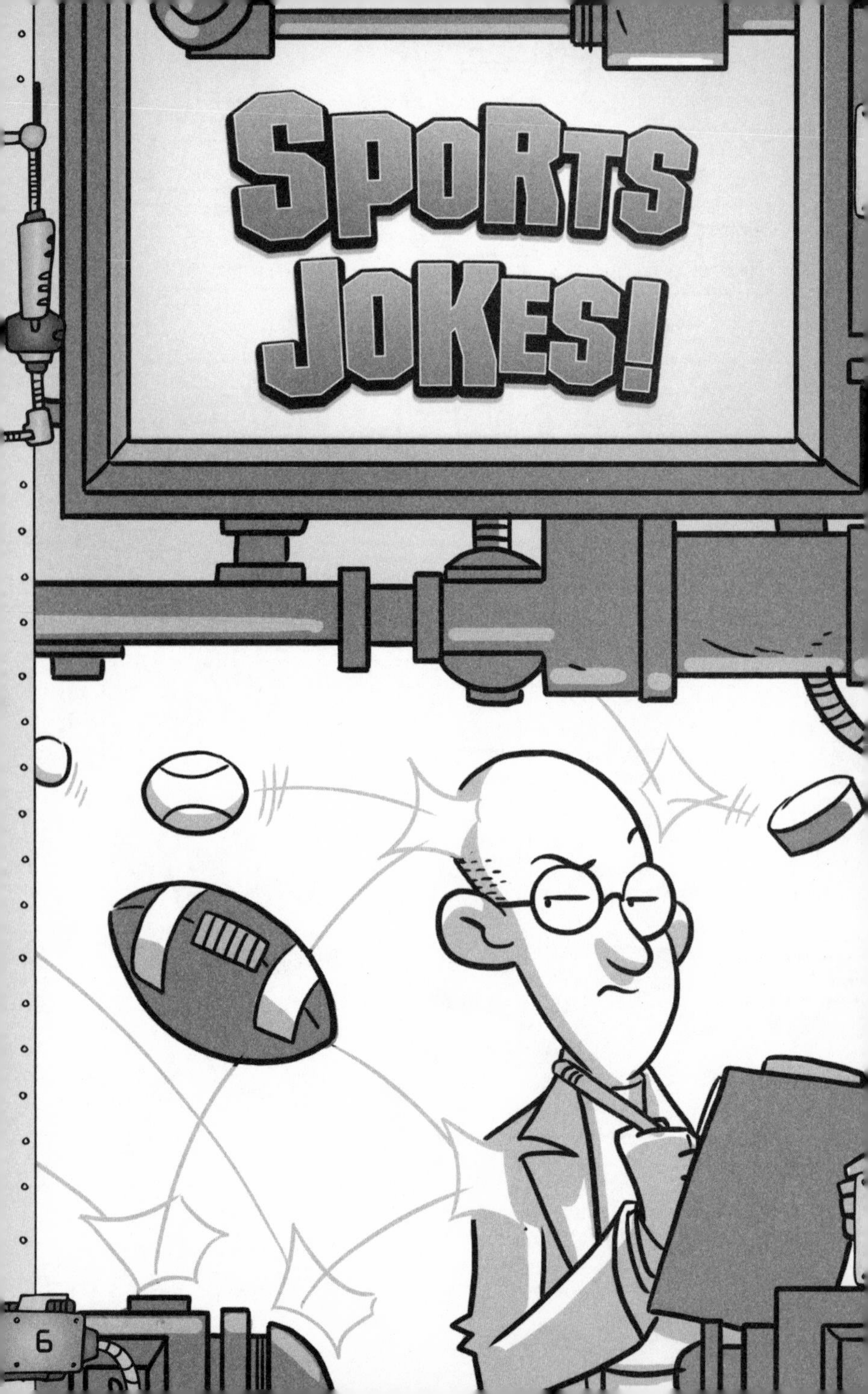
SPORTS JOKES!

Why was Cinderella thrown off the soccer team?

Because she ran away from the ball.

What do you call a pig that knows karate?

A pork chop!

What do you call a basketball player's pet chicken?

A personal fowl.

Why was Cinderella so bad at gymnastics?
Because she had a pumpkin for a coach.

What kind of cats like to go bowling?
Alley cats.

Did you hear about the race between the lettuce and the banana?

The lettuce was a head.

Who won the race between the two ocean waves?

They tide.

Where do golfers go after a game?

To a tee party.

Why shouldn't skaters tell jokes when they're racing?

Because the ice might crack up!

What did one soccer shoe say to the other?
Between us we're gonna have a ball!

What football team travels with the most luggage?
The Packers.

What football team spends the most money on their credit cards?
The Chargers.

A soccer player and a duck went out to dinner at a restaurant. But after dessert, the soccer player kicked the duck.
Why?
He said he would foot the bill.

Why is a baseball stadium always so cool?

Because it's full of fans.

What dessert should basketball players never eat?

Turnovers.

What mammal always shows up at a baseball game?

A bat.

Why didn't the golfer wear his new shoes on the golf course?

Because yesterday he got a hole in one.

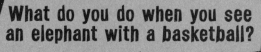

What do you do when you see an elephant with a basketball?

Get out of his way!

What is the quietest sport in the world?
Bowling. You can hear a pin drop!

What game do sheep like playing?
Baaa-dminton.

What did the coach say to the broken candy machine?

Give me my quarterback!

What has 18 legs and catches flies?

A baseball team.

What is the hardest part about sky-diving?

The ground!

Why is tennis such a noisy game?

Because the players always raise a racket!

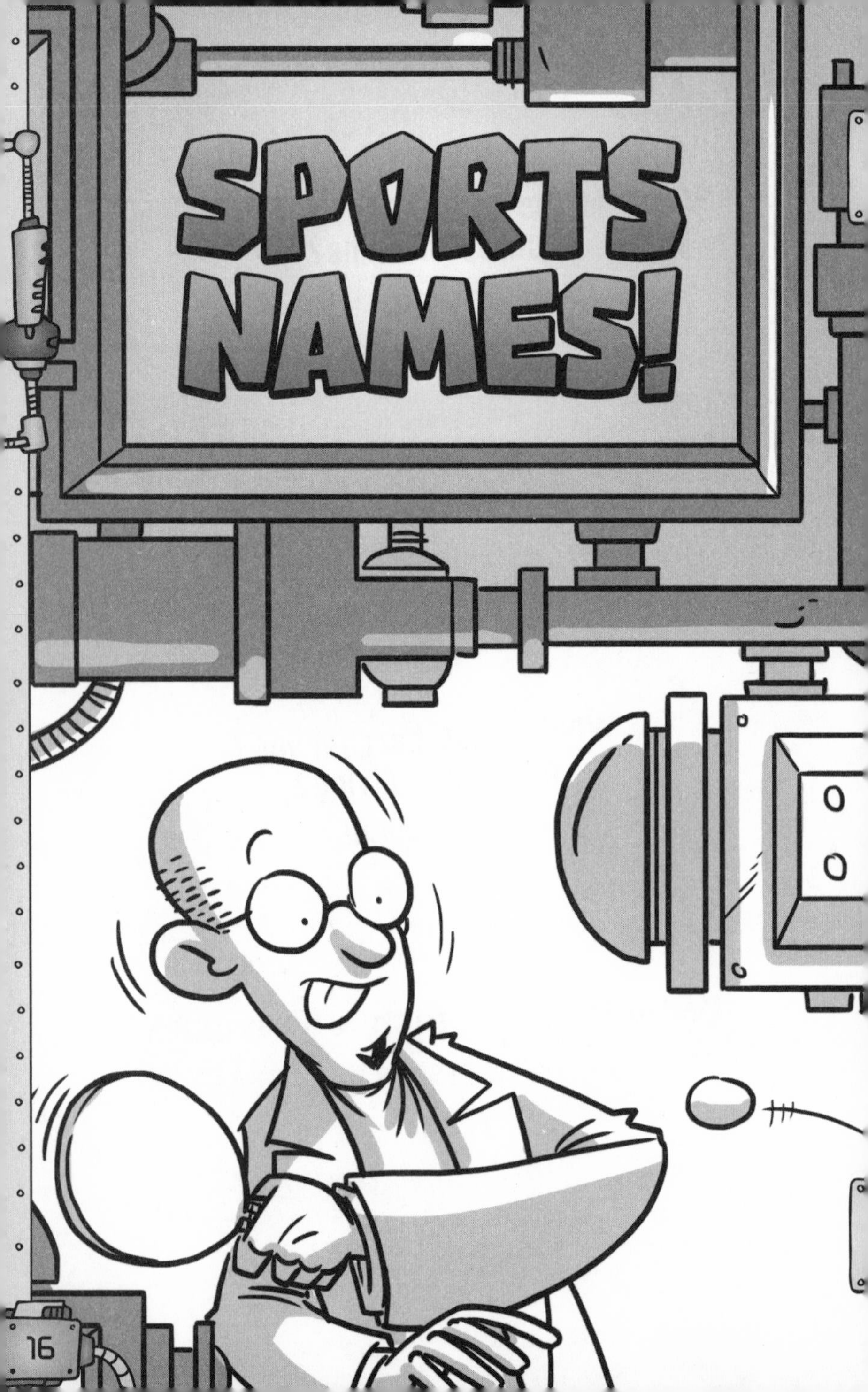
SPORTS NAMES!

What do you call a guy who's good at wrestling?

MATT

What do you call a girl who's good at fishing?

ANNETTE

What do you call a guy who's great at scoring in volleyball?

SPIKE

What do you call a girl who's at the start of every boxing match?

BELLE

What do you call a guy who's good at catching fly balls?

MITT

What do you call a guy who's good at archery?

BO

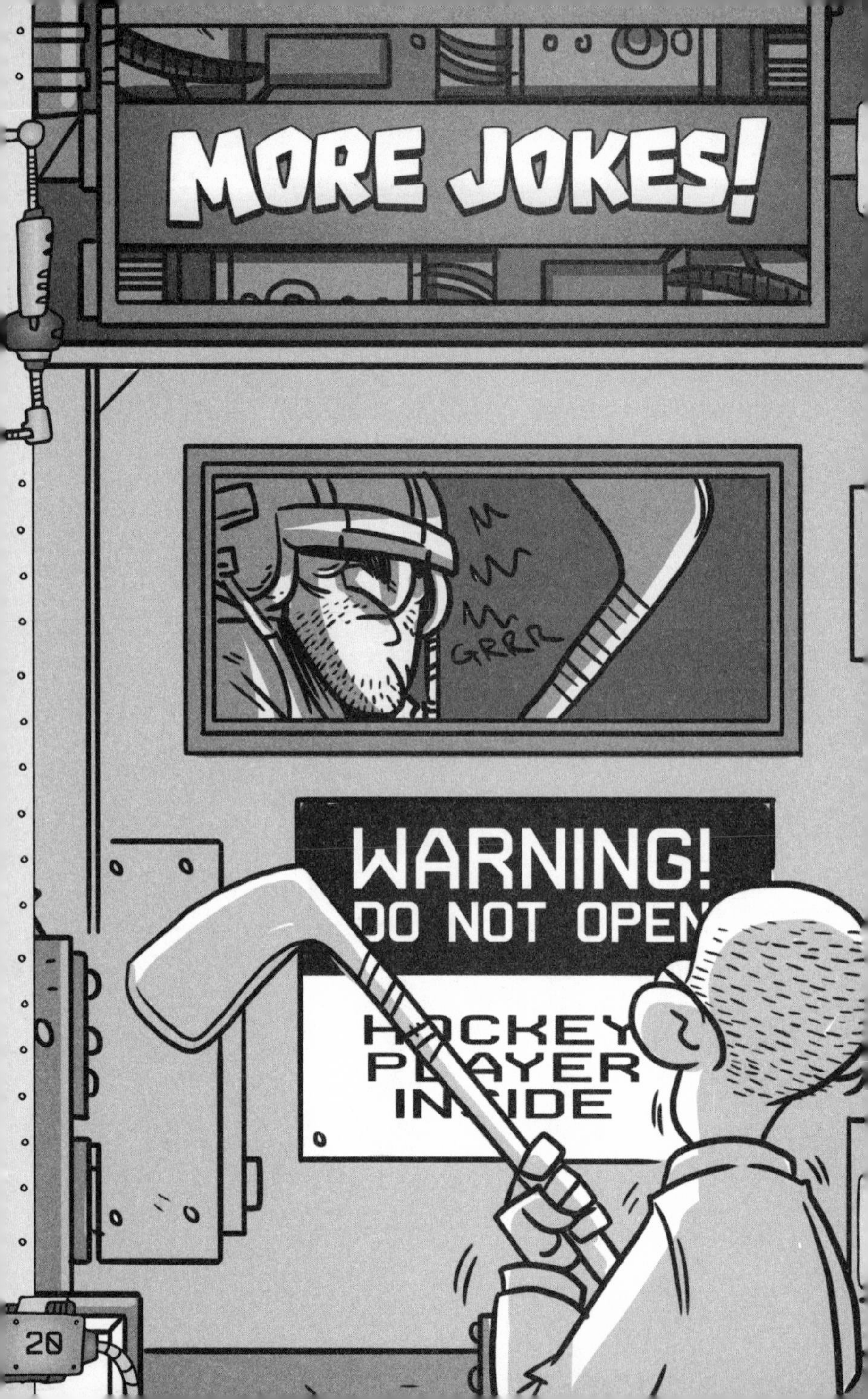
MORE JOKES!
GRRR
WARNING!
DO NOT OPEN
HOCKEY
PLAYER
INSIDE

Why shouldn't a basketball player write a check?

Because it will probably bounce.

Why did the baseball hitter spend so much time at the playground?

He was working on his swing.

What famous baseball player lives under a tree?

Babe Root.

Which player on a basketball team has the best sense of smell?

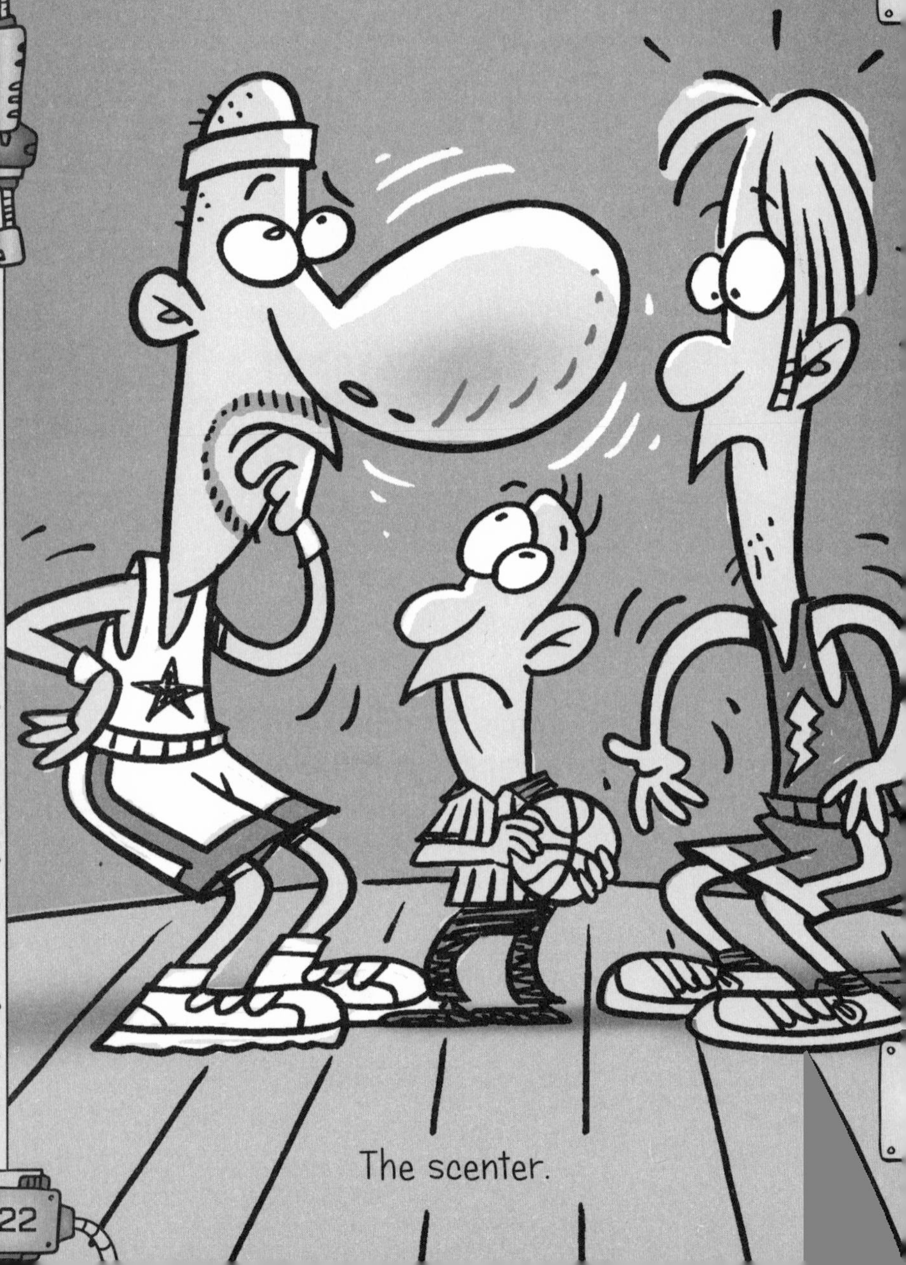

The scenter.

How is a hockey player like a magician?
They both do hat tricks!

Why are fish so bad at playing tennis?
They always run when they see a net!

Who's big, is a lumberjack, and runs marathons?
I give up.
Paul Bunion.

What do boxers and fishermen have in common?

They both land a hook in the jaw!

Never stand in front of an Olympic hurler.

Why, cuz I might get hit by the ball?

No, because he just had lunch!

What bird is good at boxing?

Duck.

Why did the bowling pins lie down?

They were on strike!

What position does Frankenstein play in hockey?

Ghoul keeper.

What is a cheerleader's favorite color?

Yeller!

Why is the receiver digging a pit in the middle of the football field?

The quarterback told him to "Go deep!"

Why did the tennis player carry a flashlight?

Because he always lost his matches!

What is the world's oldest sport?

Baseball. The Bible's first words are "In the big inning . . ."

Where do they serve food to football players?

In the Soup-er Bowl.

Where did the relay-racer wash his shoes?

In running water.

Why did the piano player join the baseball team?

Because he had perfect pitch.

Why was the nose so sad when his friends divided up into soccer teams?

Because it didn't get picked.

What do librarians take with them when they go fishing?

Bookworms!

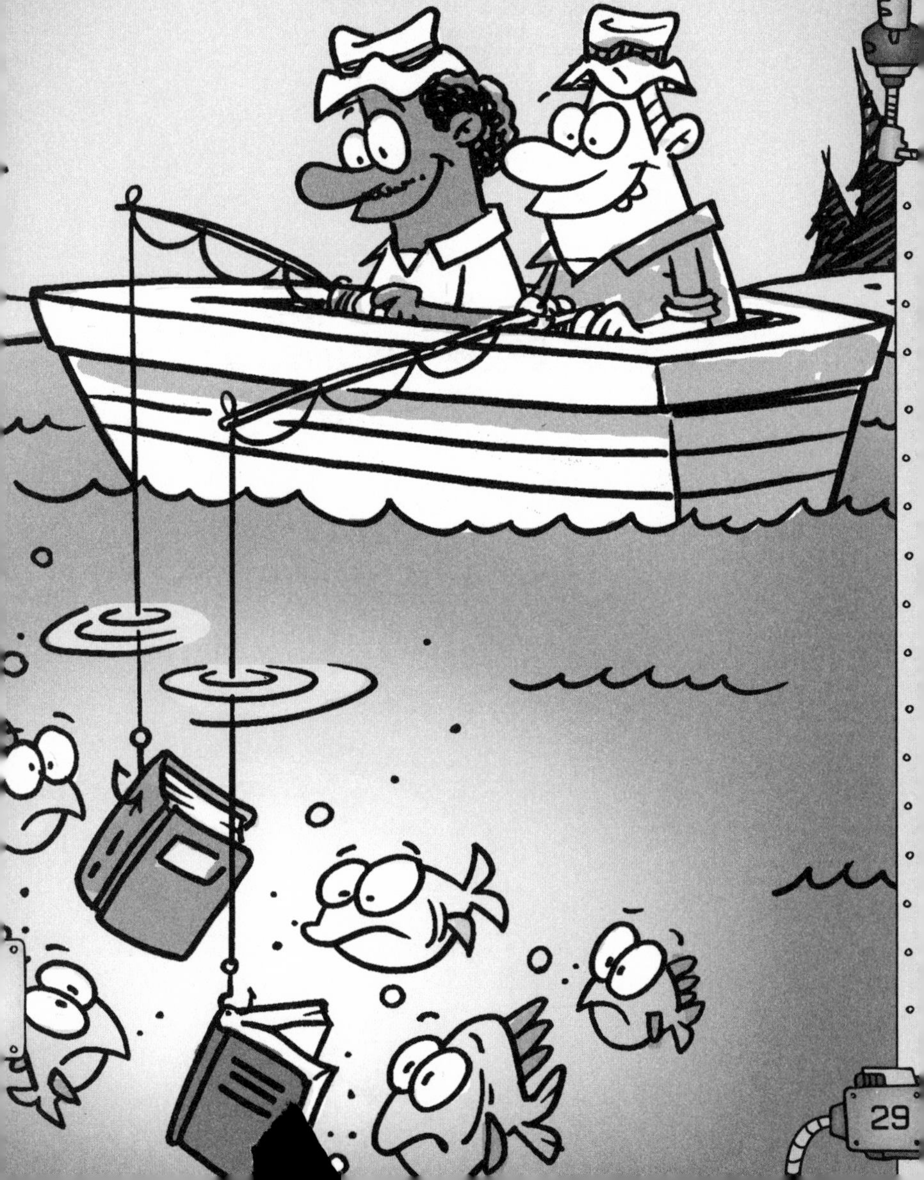

**What did the football player
say when he grabbed
the duck?**

"Touch down!"

**How is a skydiver like a big
game hunter?**

They both like to chute.

**What is harder to catch the
faster you run?**

Your breath!

When is a baby good at basketball?

When she's dribbling!

What do you call a pig who plays basketball?

A ball hog.

Why did the baseball owner hire elephants for his team?

Because they work for peanuts.

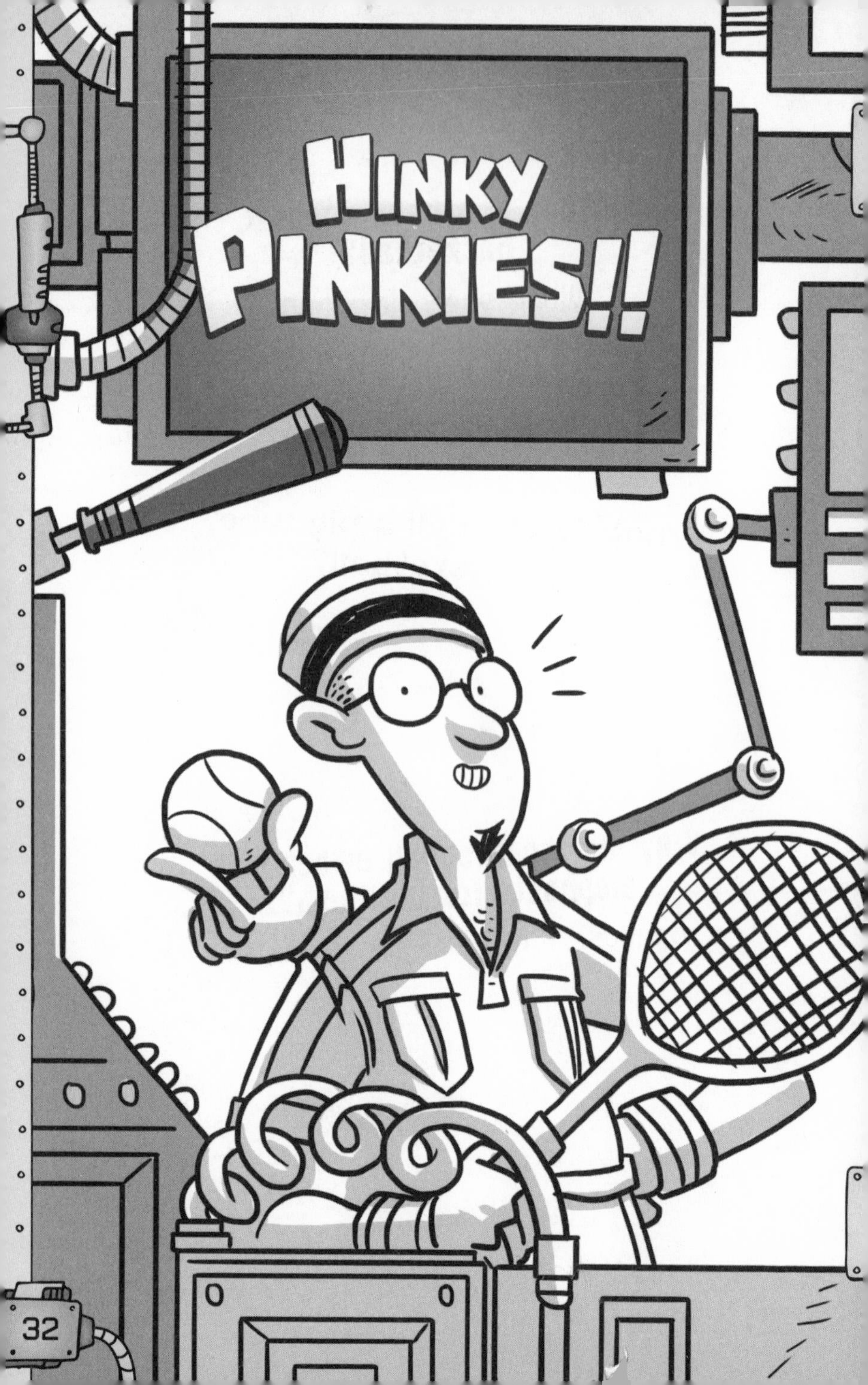
HINKY PINKIES!!

What do you call an astronaut who plays first base?

A SPACEMAN BASEMAN

What do you call a soccer player made of Swiss cheese?

A HOLEY GOALIE

What do you call
a wrestling match
between two pumped-
up fighters?

A MUSCLE TUSSLE

What do you call slime
on a basketball?

HOOP GOOP

What do you call a skateboarder who serves you dinner?

A SKATER WAITER

What do you call someone who pulls the football away at the very last moment?

A KICKER TRICKER

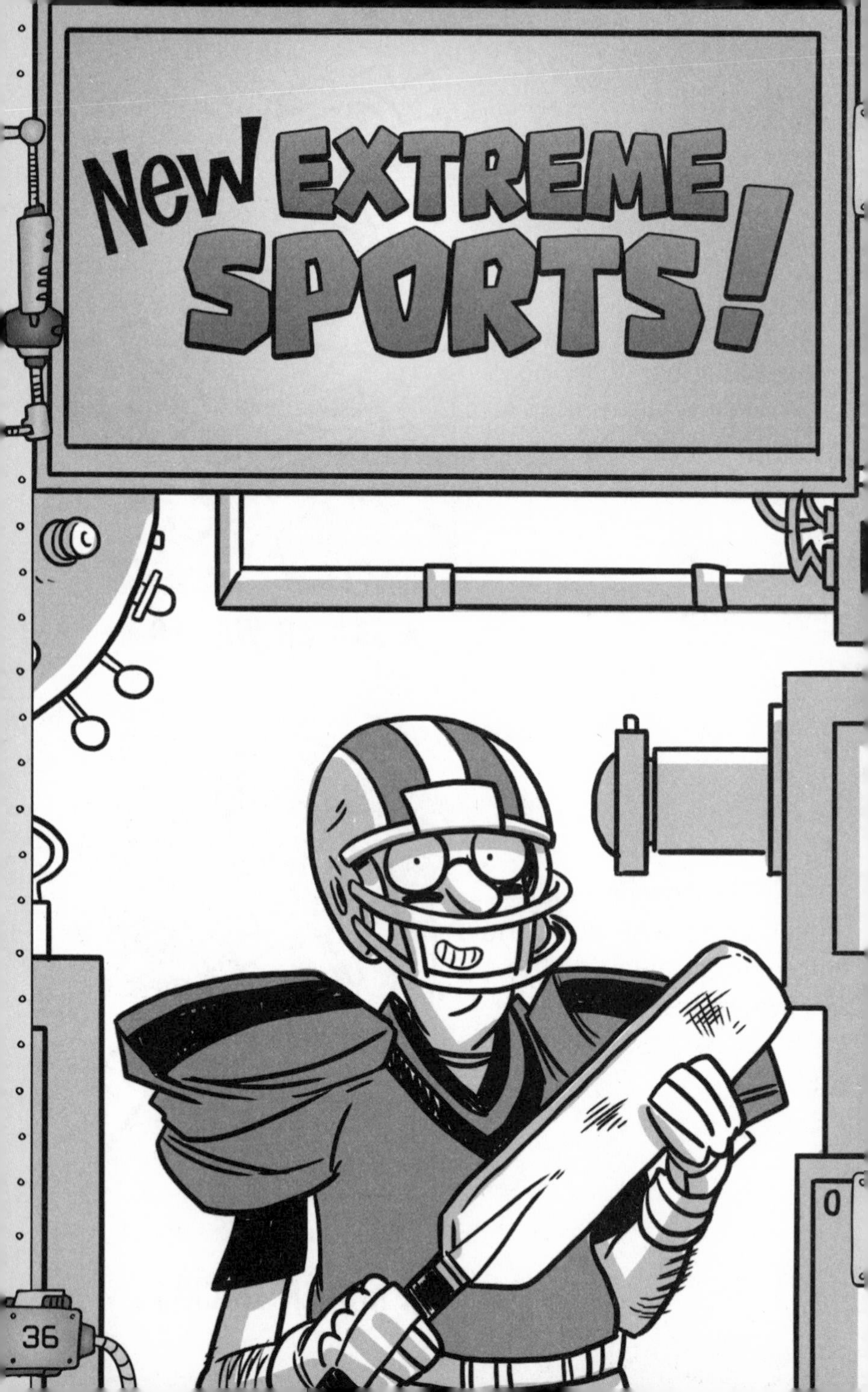
New EXTREME SPORTS!

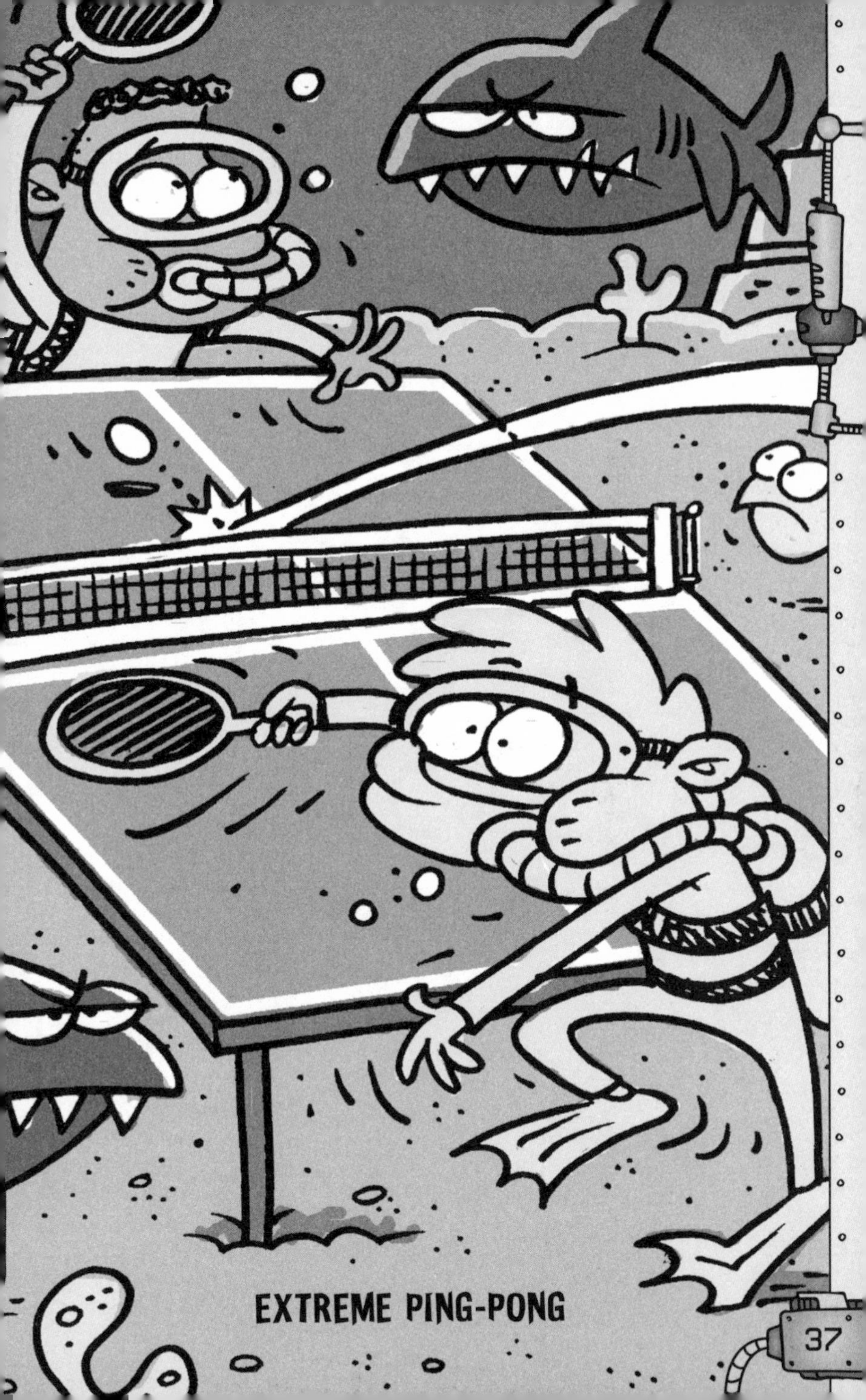

EXTREME PING-PONG

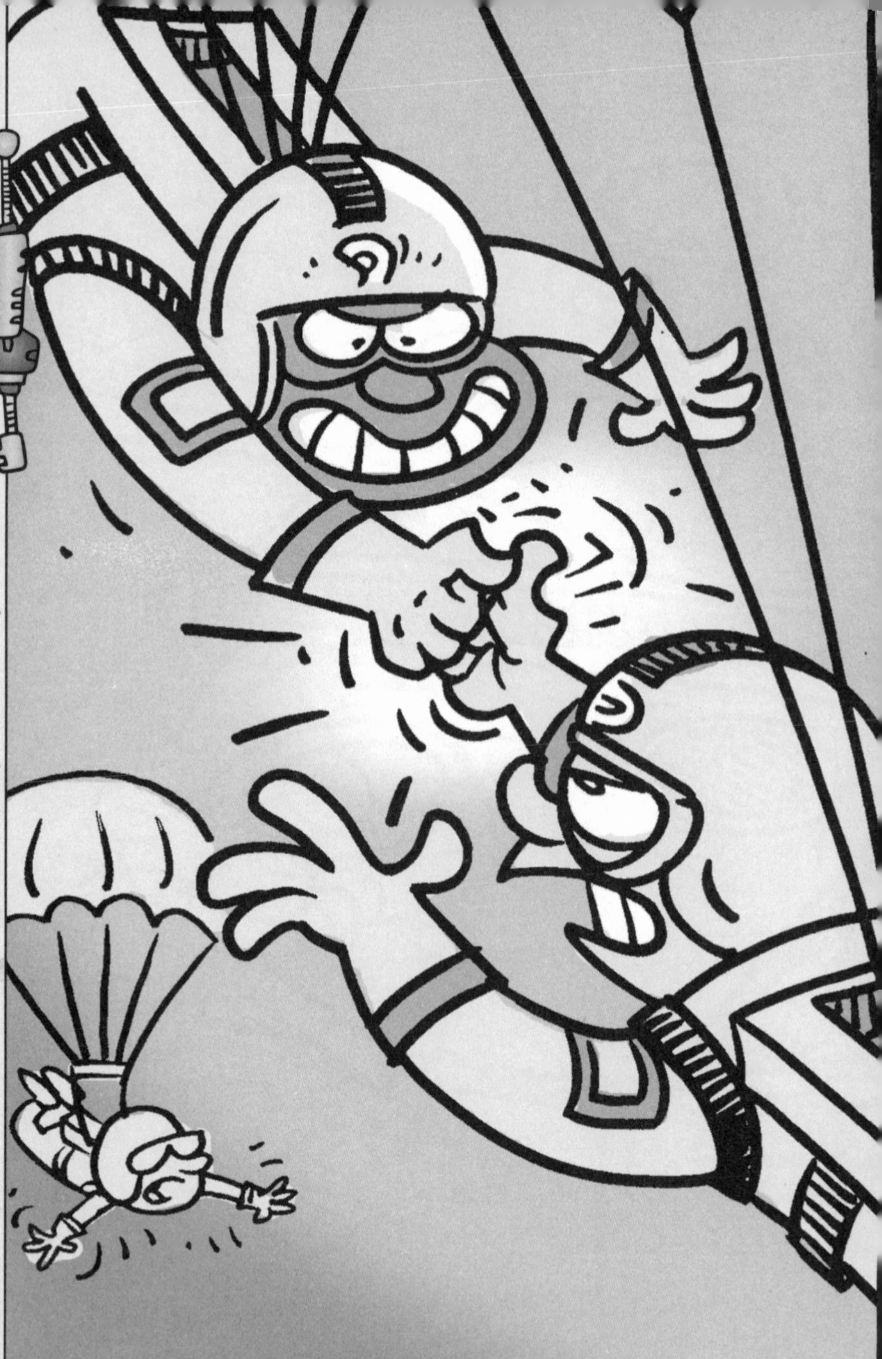

EXTREME THUMB WRESTLING

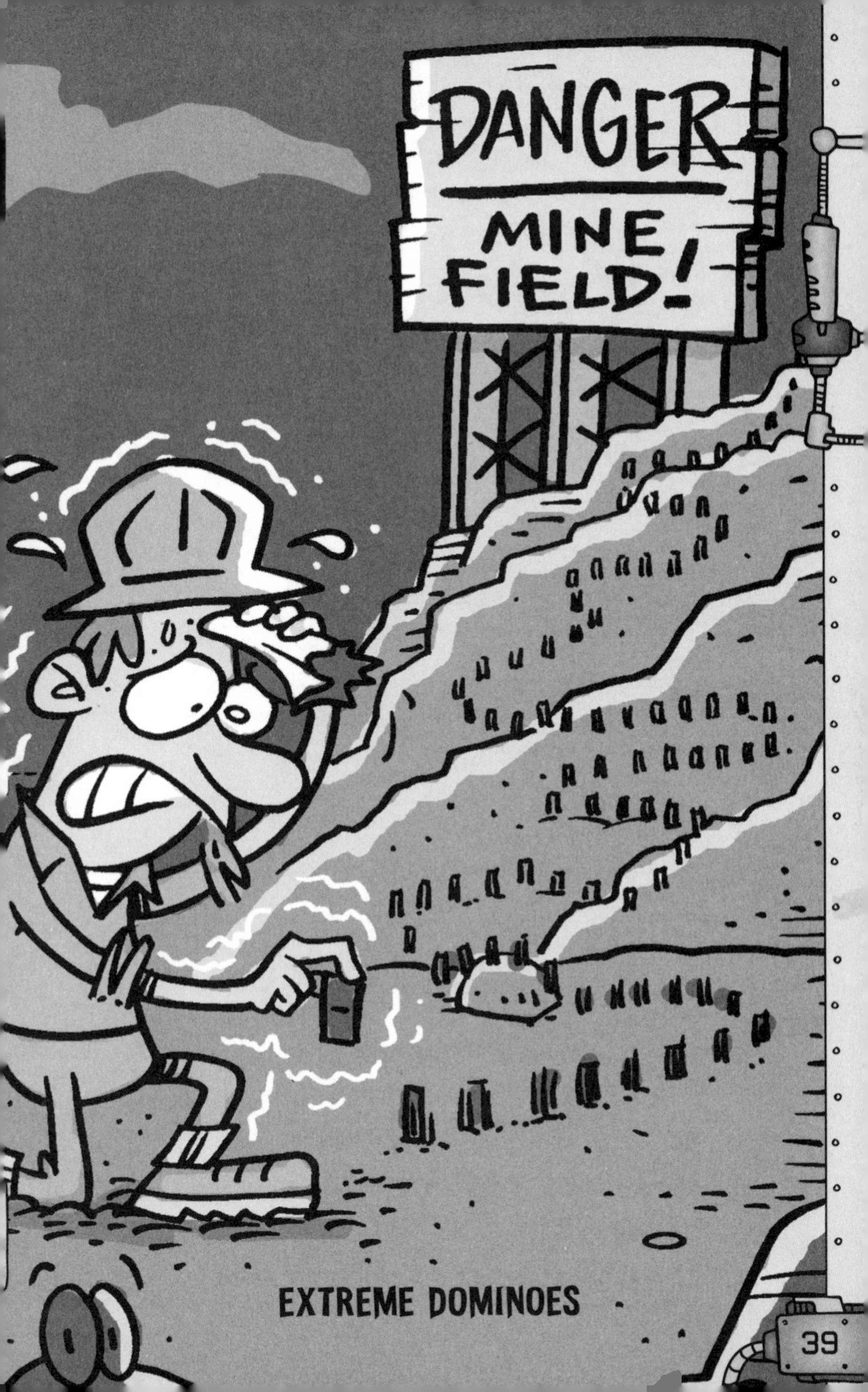
DANGER
MINE FIELD!

EXTREME DOMINOES

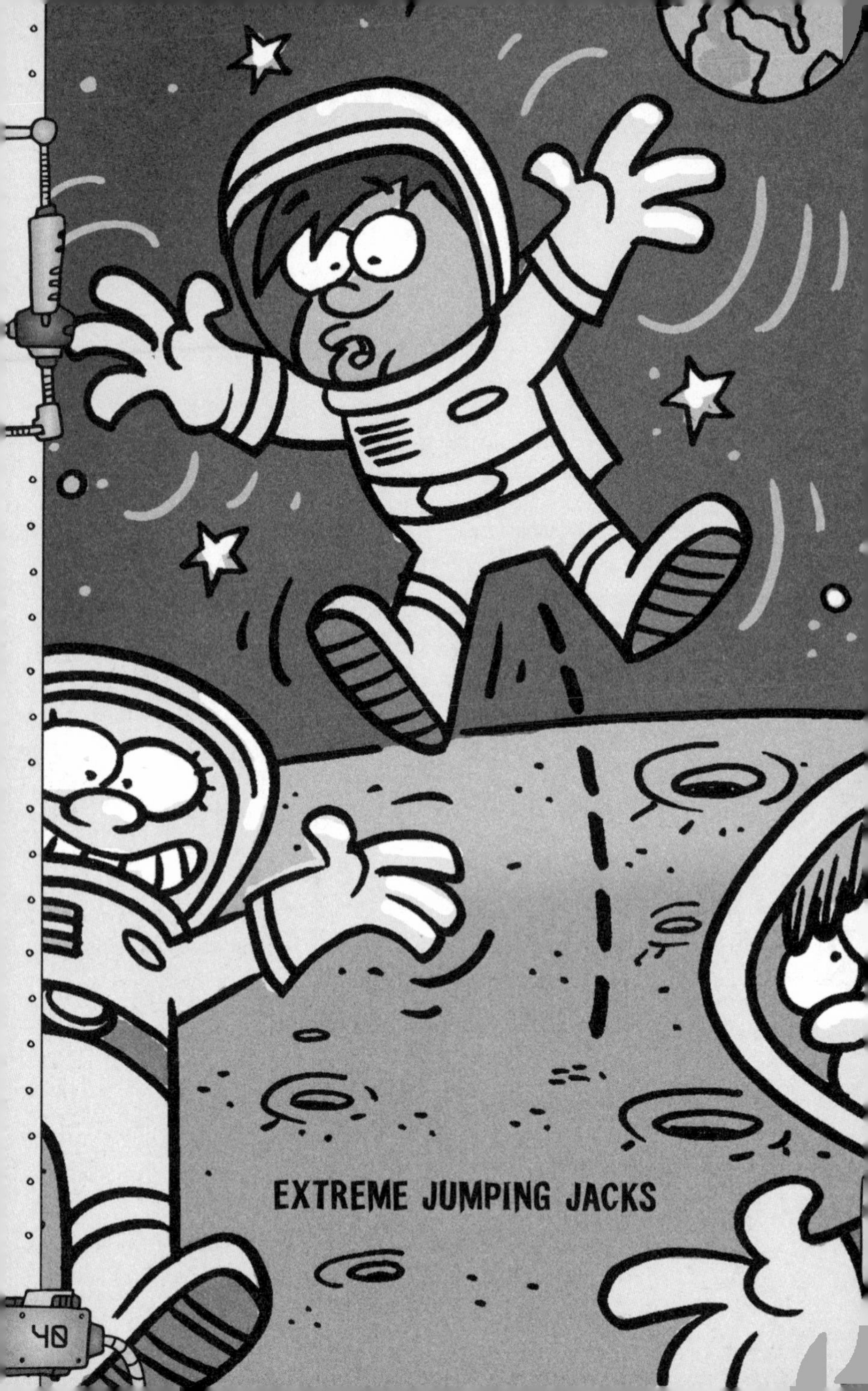
EXTREME JUMPING JACKS

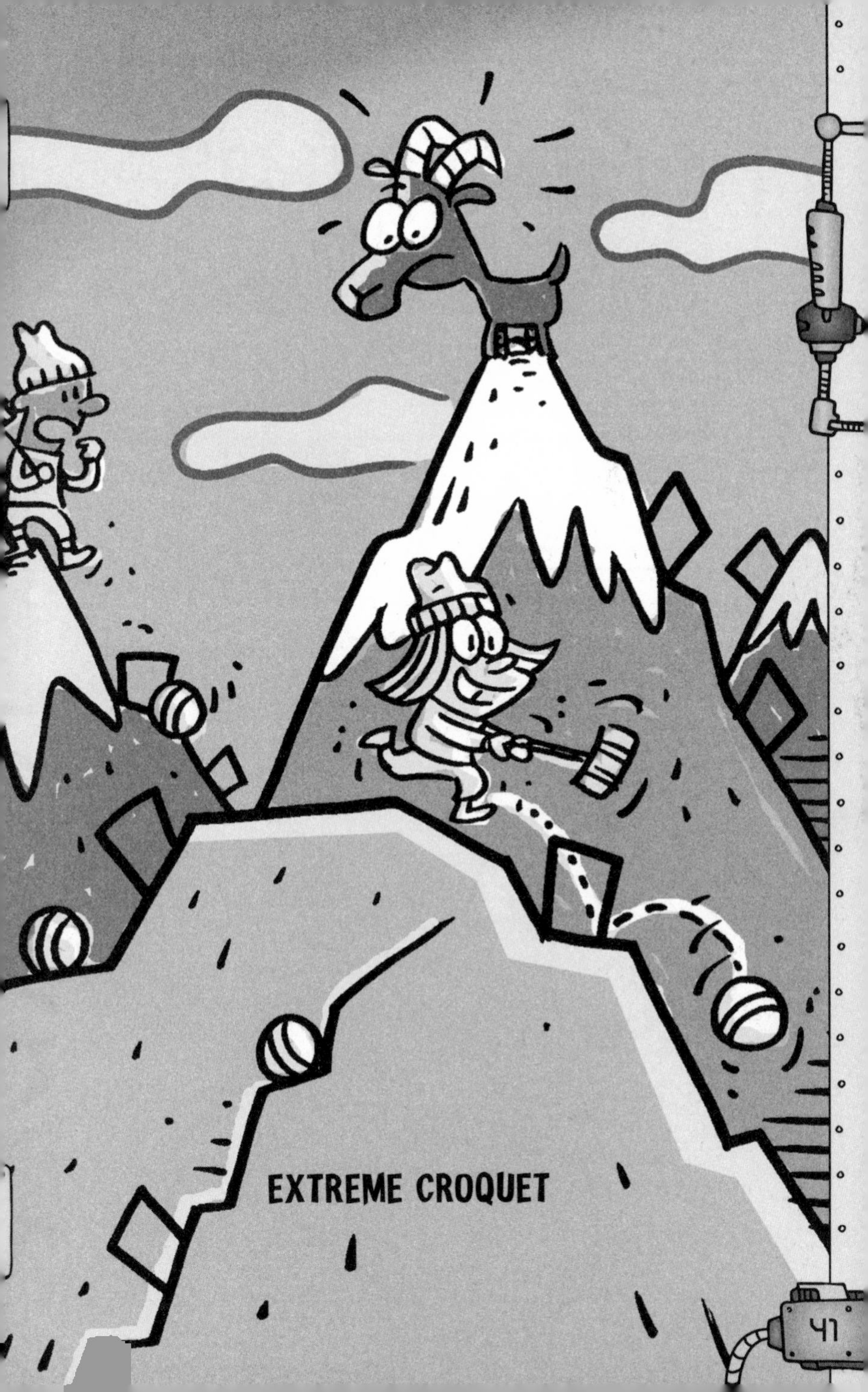
EXTREME CROQUET

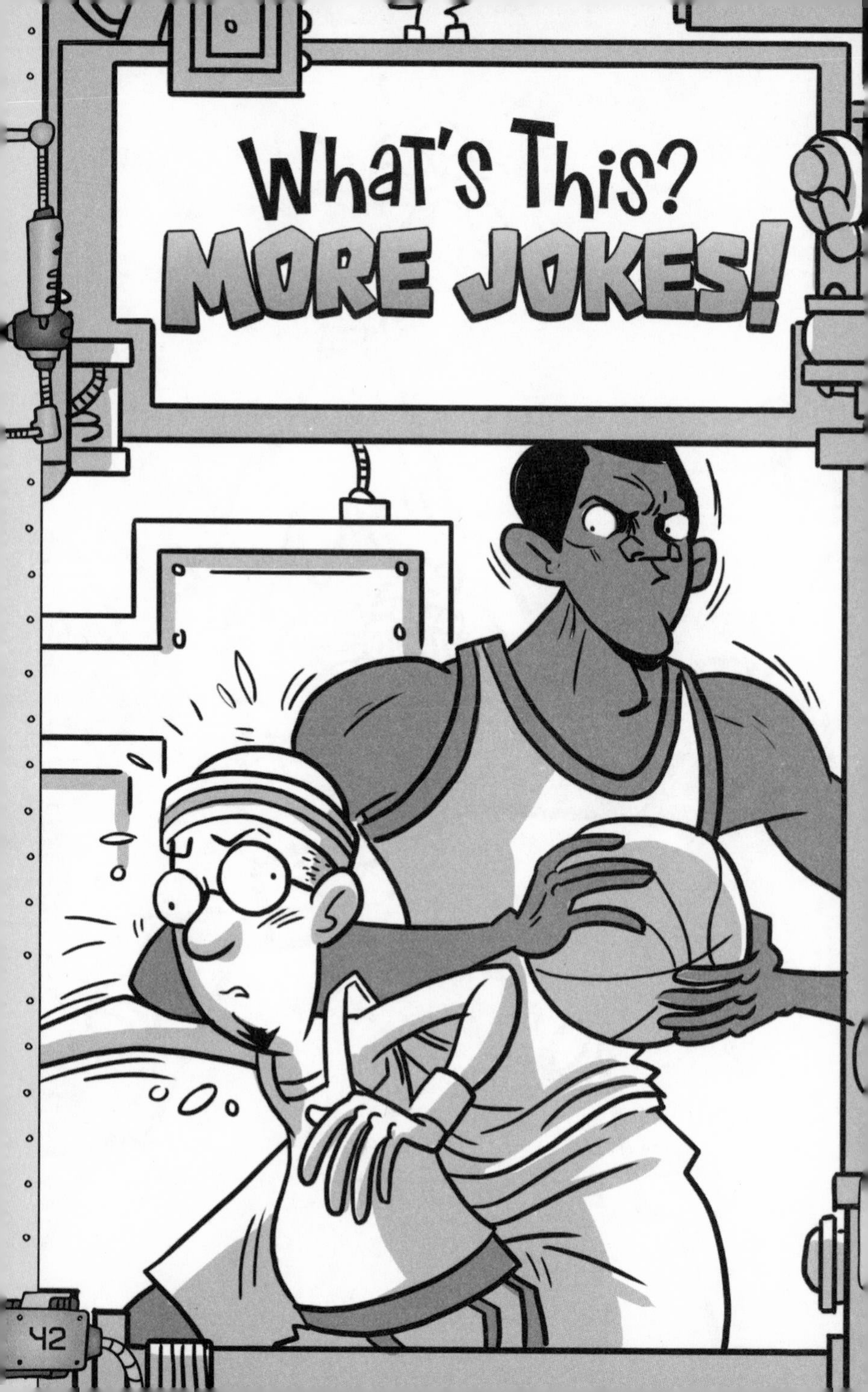
What's This?
MORE JOKES!

What do you call a boomerang that doesn't work?

A stick.

Why did the ballerina quit?

It was tu-tu hard!

What country holds the most marathons?

Iran.

Why are bullfights so noisy?

The bulls are always using their horns!

How do fireflies start a race?
"Ready. Set. Glow!"

Do you ever go rock climbing?
I would if I were boulder!

What is a runner's favorite subject in school?

Jography.

Why did the softball player bring her bat to the library?

Her teacher told her to hit the books!

Where can you find the largest diamond in the world?

On a baseball field.

What lights up a sports stadium?
A soccer match.

Which state has the most football uniforms?
New Jersey!

That robot must be a super athlete.
How can you tell?
Look at the size of that metal on his chest!

Where do elephants exercise?

At the jungle gym.

What do you call it when a T. rex makes a home run?

A dinoscore!

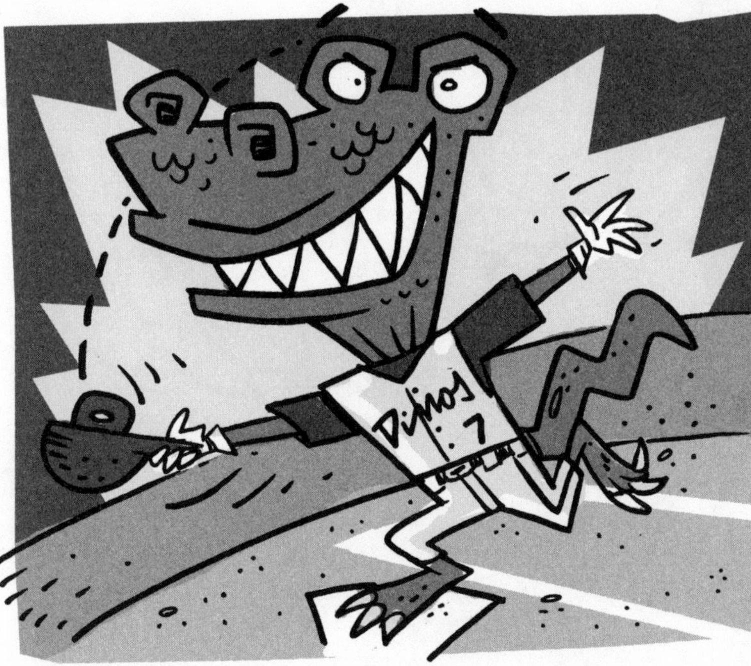
Dinos
7

Why do soccer players get good grades?

They're always using their heads.

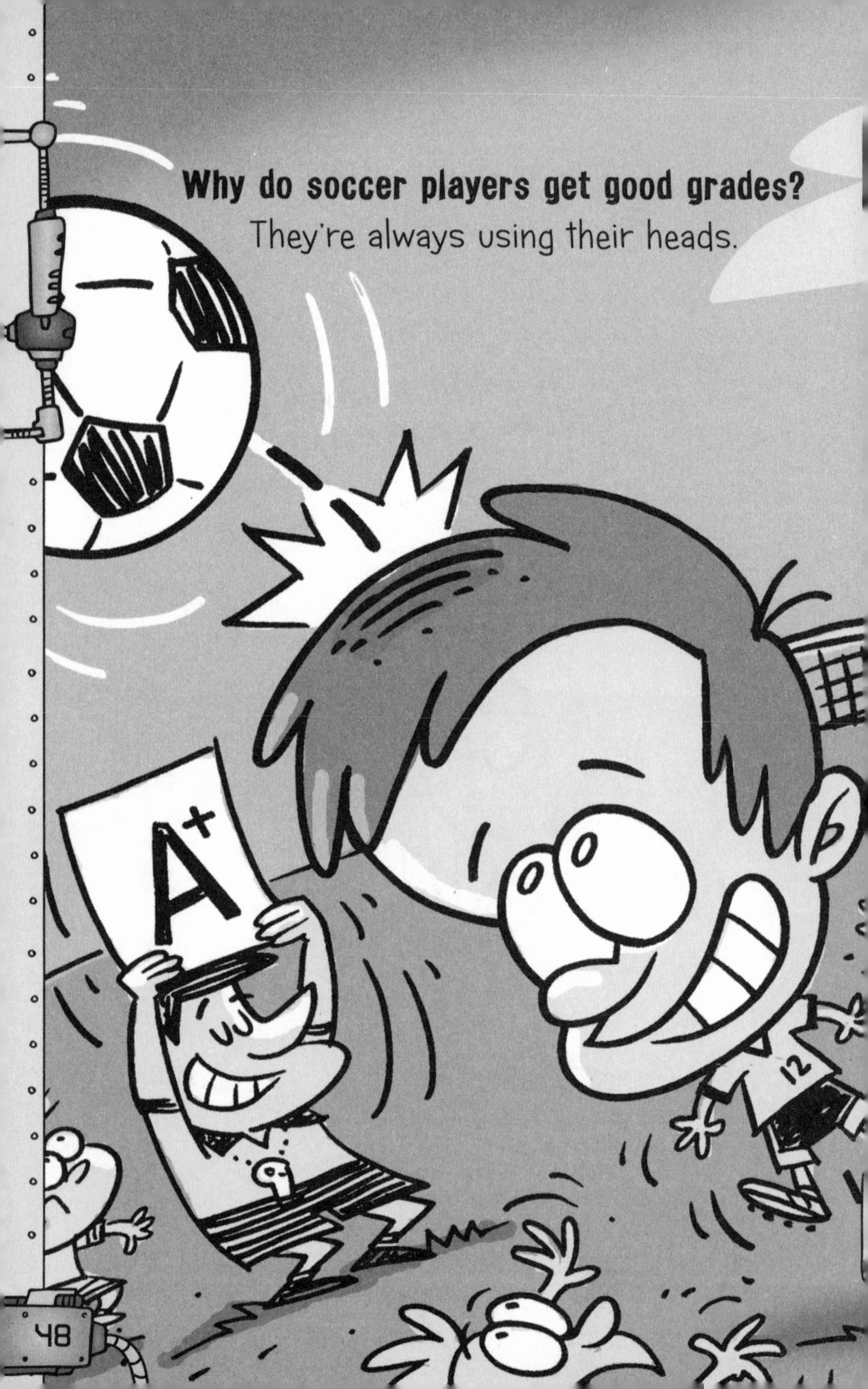
A+
12

Why did the referee stop the zombie hockey game?

There was a face off in the corner.

Why couldn't the motorcycle racer pass the 18-wheeler?

Because it was two-tired!

What did the baseball glove say to the baseball?

"Catch you later."

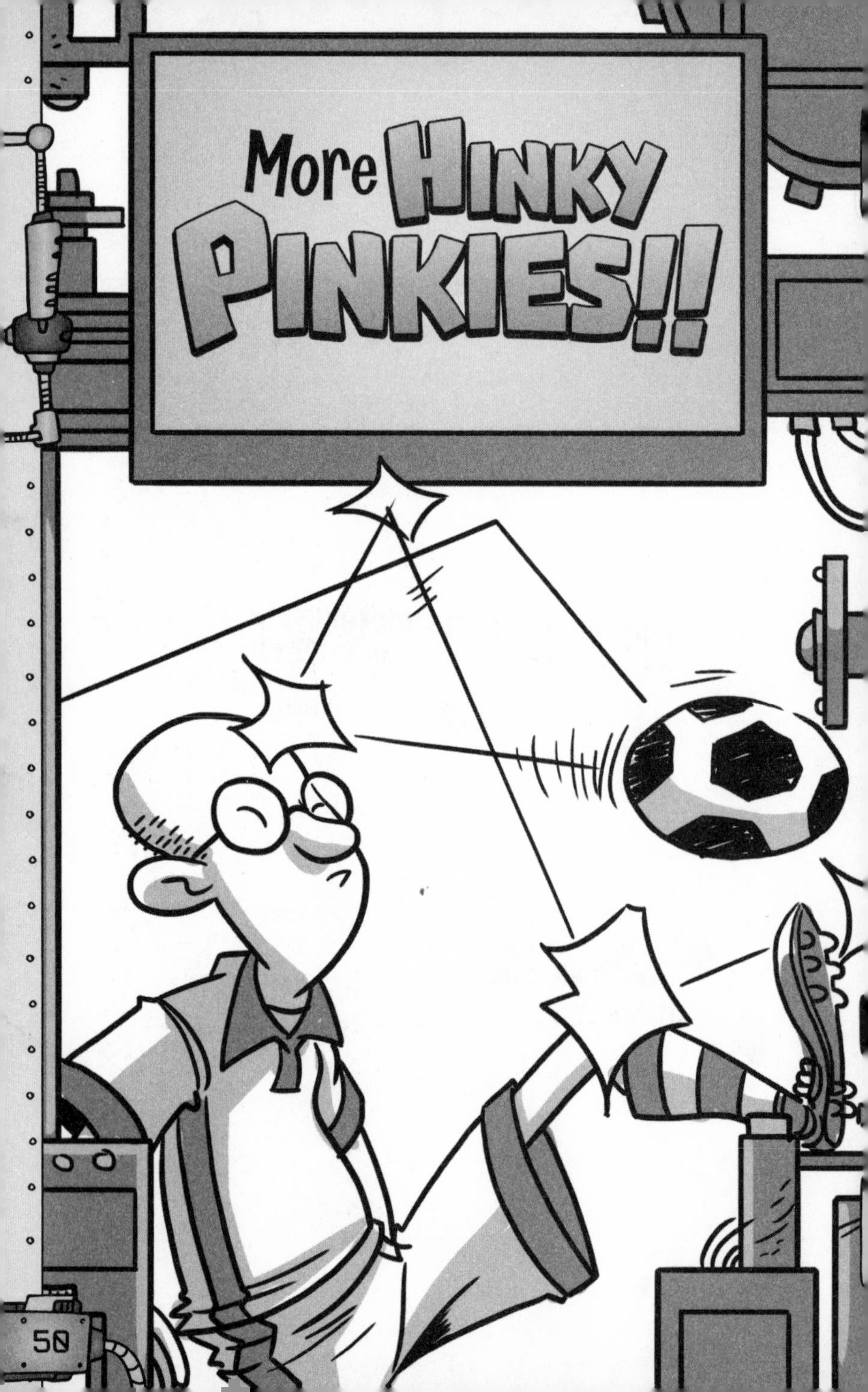
More HINKY PINKIES!!

What do you call the special move to avoid getting brained during a hockey game?

A PUCK DUCK

What equipment do underwater volleyball players use?

A WET NET

What do you call a rip in a baseball glove?

A MITT SPLIT

What do you call a lot of noise on the tennis court?

A RACQUET RACKET

What do you call the baseball player at homeplate who gets run over by a steamroller?

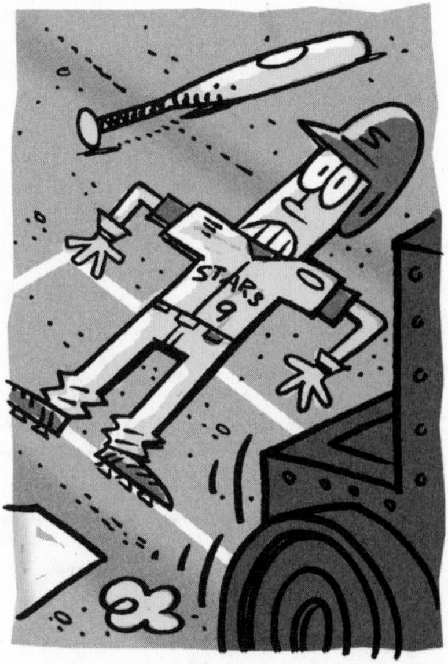
STARS
9

THE FLATTER BATTER

What kind of race does a tortoise run at the Olympics?

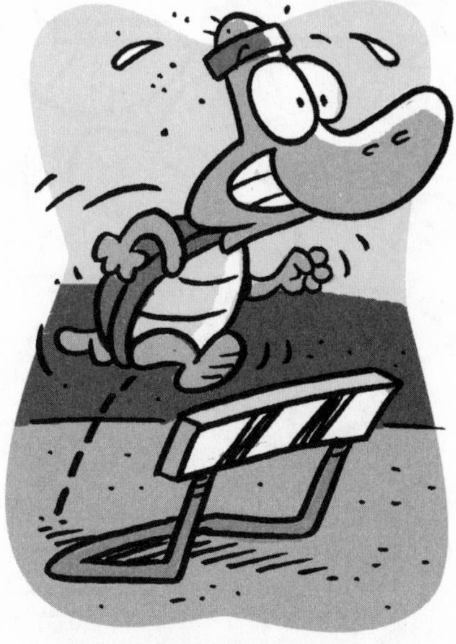

A TURTLE HURDLE

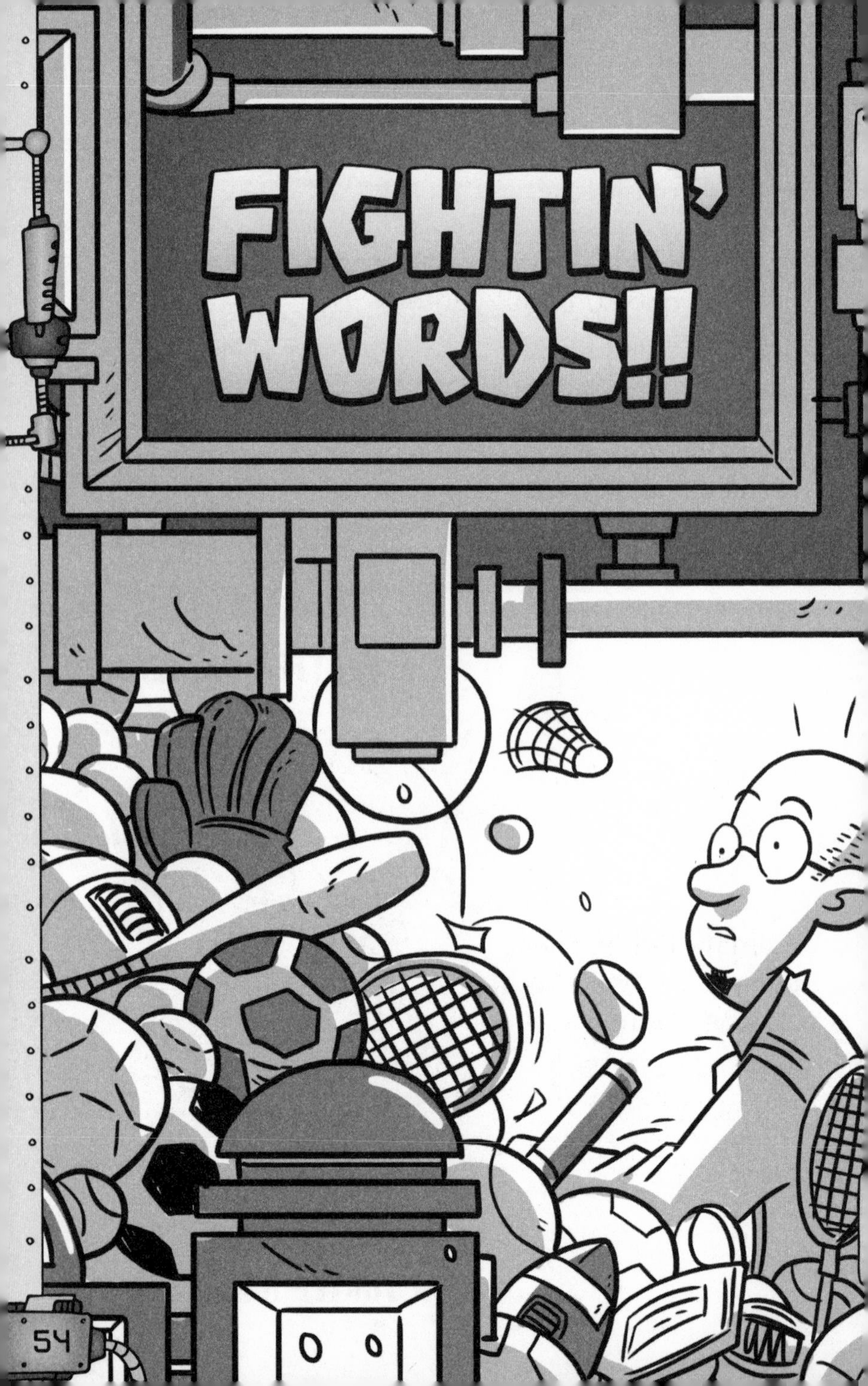
FIGHTIN' WORDS!!

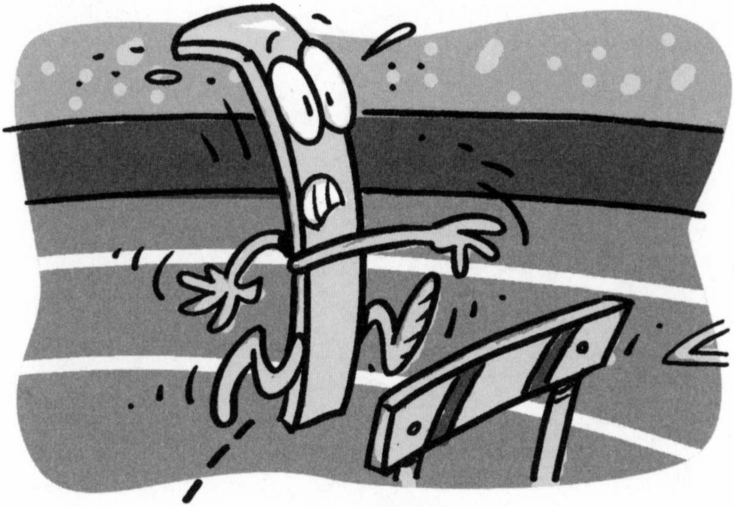

SKI JUMP

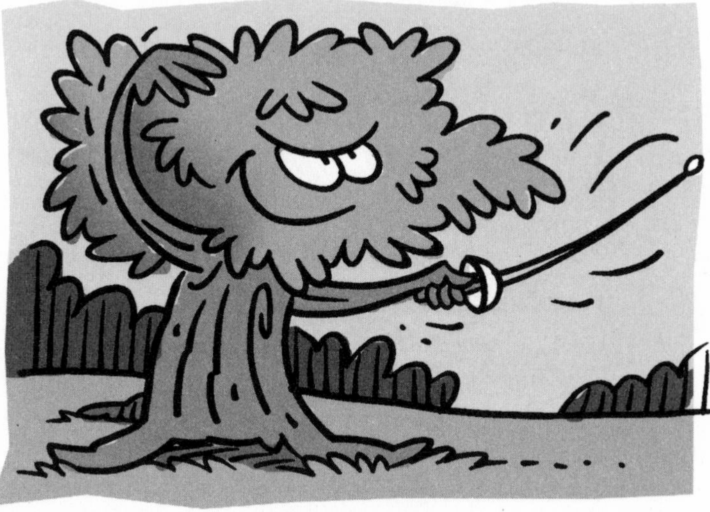

WOOD FENCE

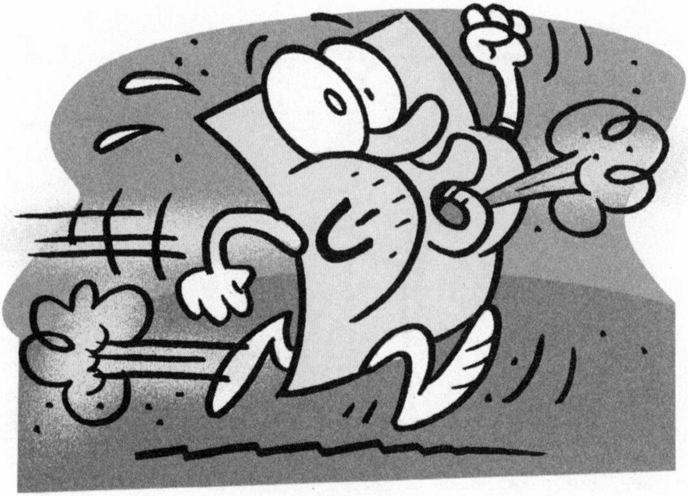

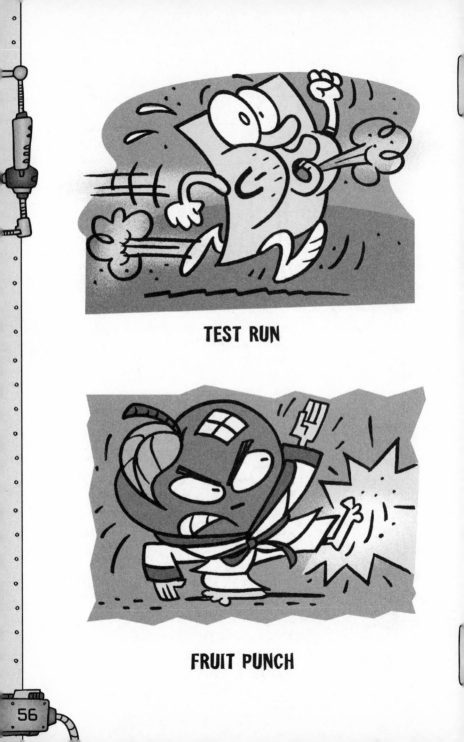

TEST RUN

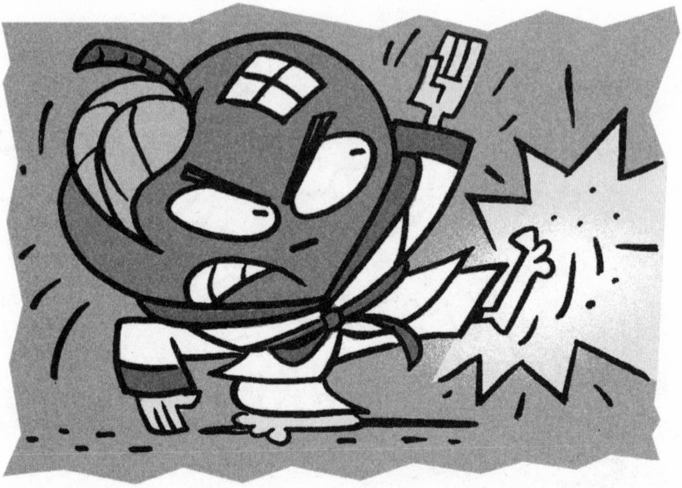

FRUIT PUNCH

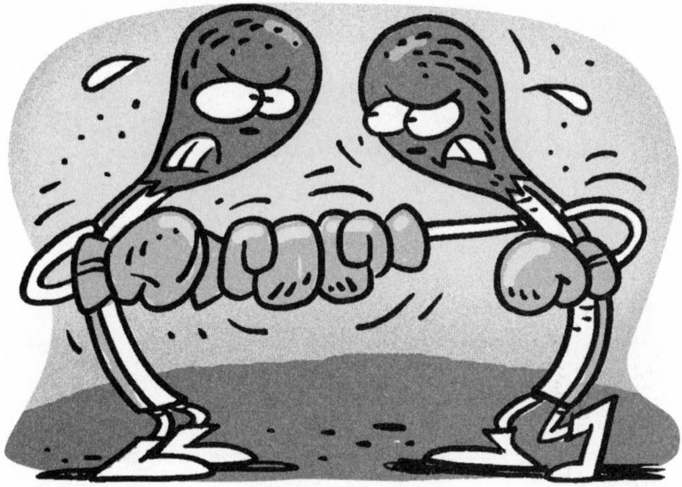

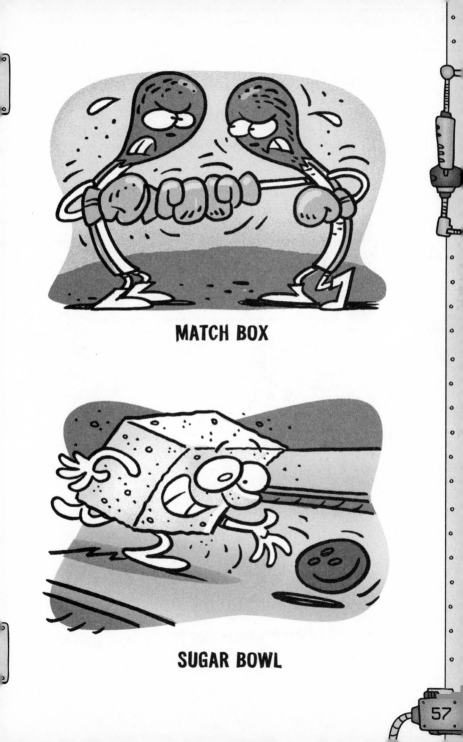

MATCH BOX

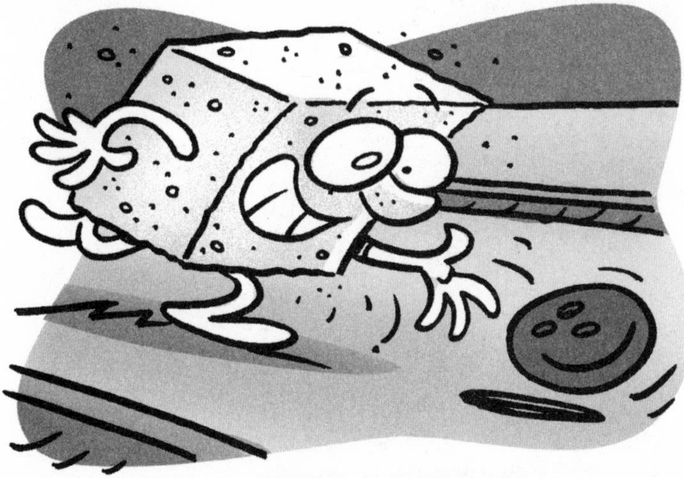

SUGAR BOWL

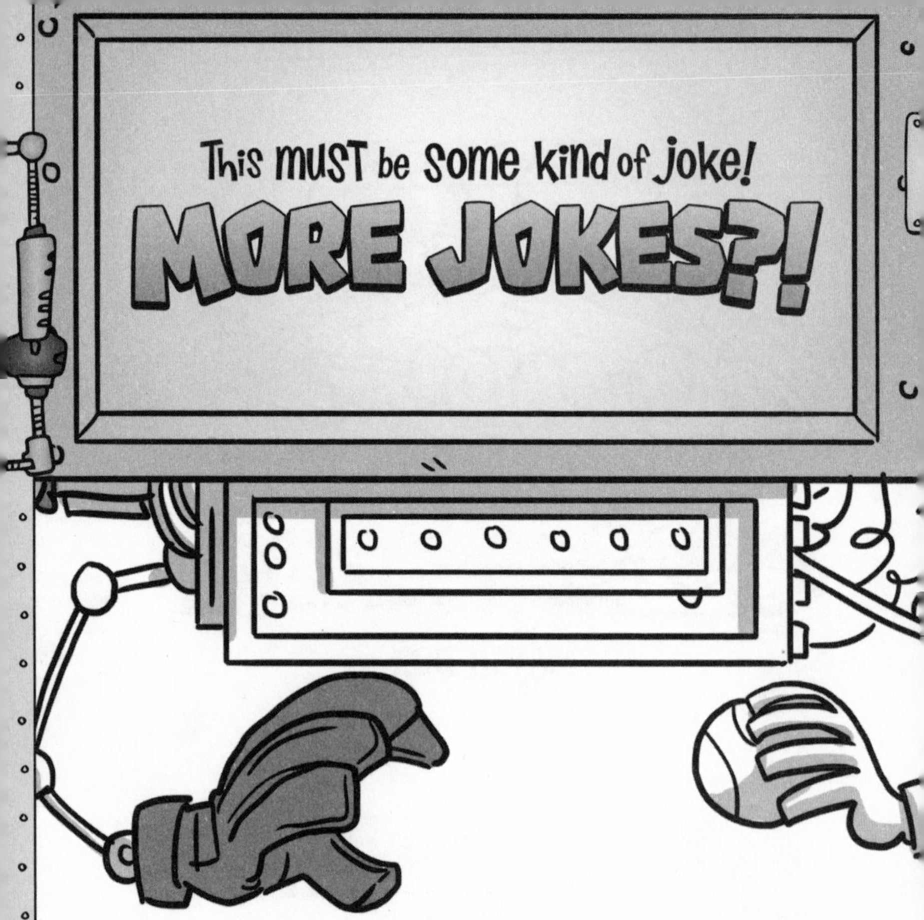
This MUST be some kind of joke!
MORE JOKES?!

What position did the barbed wire play on the football team?

De-fence!

Why did the baseball team put a trampoline on first base?

For spring training.

What sport do dogs like to play?
Biscuit ball.

Why was the baseball pitcher wearing armor?
It was a knight game!

How does a quarterback spend his free time in the outdoors?
Hiking.

I think a baseball player lives in that house. How can you tell?

The front door has a welcome mitt.

Where do baseball players eat?

On home plate.

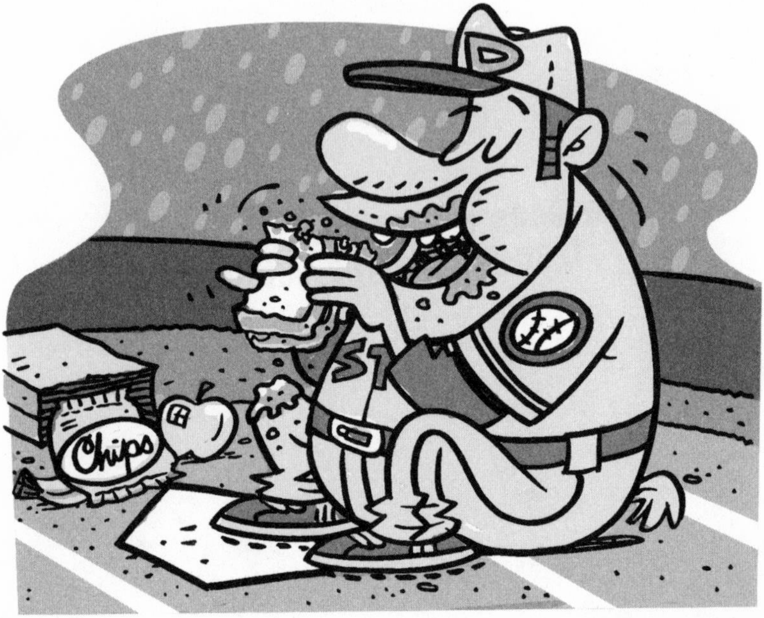
Chips

How do basketball players cool off during a game?

They stand near the fans!

Why didn't the dog want to play on the wrestling team?

Because it was a boxer!

What country has the world's fastest runners?

Rush-a!

How is a softball team like a pancake?
They both need a good batter!

How does a nuclear scientist stay in shape?
By pumping ion!

Kid #1: My baby brother is really good at basketball.

Kid #2: Really?

Kid #1: Yeah, you should see him dribble!

Knock, knock.

Who's there?

Woo.

Woo who?

Why are you cheering? We just lost the game!

Why do basketball players love donuts?
Because they get to dunk them!

Why was the golf ball so angry?
The golfer teed him off!

Why is Dracula's son so good at baseball?
Because he's a natural with bats!

Why did the wrestler bring a key to the match?

To get out of a headlock!

What is a cheerleader's favorite drink?

ROOT beer!

What is Godzilla's favorite sport?

Squash!

Why did the girl keep doing the backstroke in the pool?

She just had lunch and she didn't want to swim on a full stomach.

What sport is always getting in trouble?

Bad-minton!

What did the BMX biker say to his girlfriend?

"I wheelie wheelie like you!"

Why did the surfer wear a baseball mitt?

He wanted to catch some waves!

What did the bumble bee say when it kicked the soccer ball?

"Hive scored!"

Why was the computer so good at golf?

Because it had a hard drive!

Why did the cat get sick on the basketball court?

It had an air ball.

Why did the lawyer join the tennis team?

Because his best work is done in court.

How is a golfer like your mom doing the laundry?

They're both good at handling irons.

What do martial arts fighters eat?
Kung food!

What kind of dinosaur rides in a rodeo?
A Bronco-saurus!

That racecar driver is so boring! All he does is talk about his work.
Yeah, he has a one-track mind.

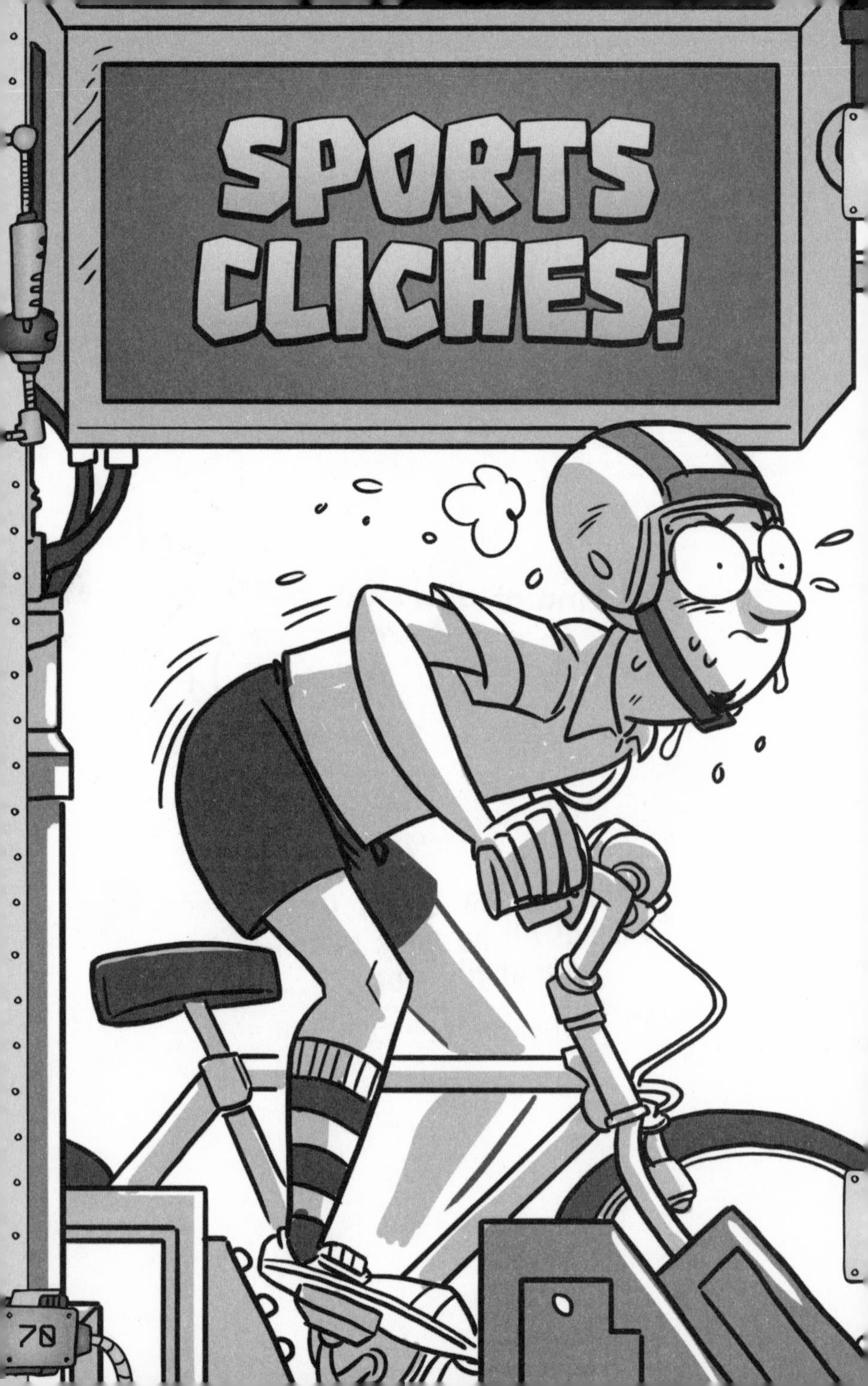
SPORTS CLICHES!

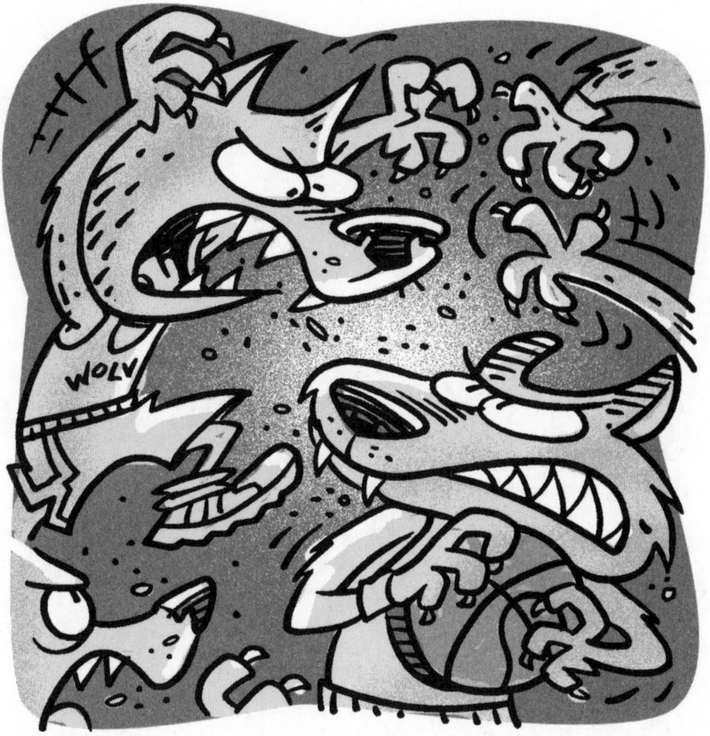
WOLV

"The teams are fighting
tooth and nail."

"The crowd is electrified."

"The referee made a good call."

"Things are starting to get ugly."

"It's a swing and a miss."

"It ain't over 'til the fat lady sings."

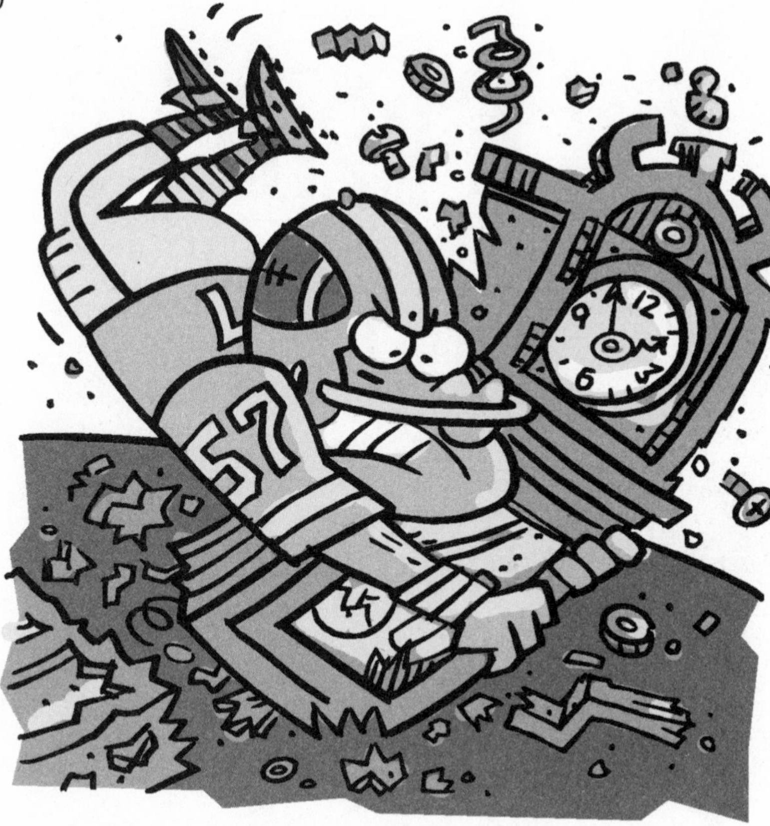
L
57

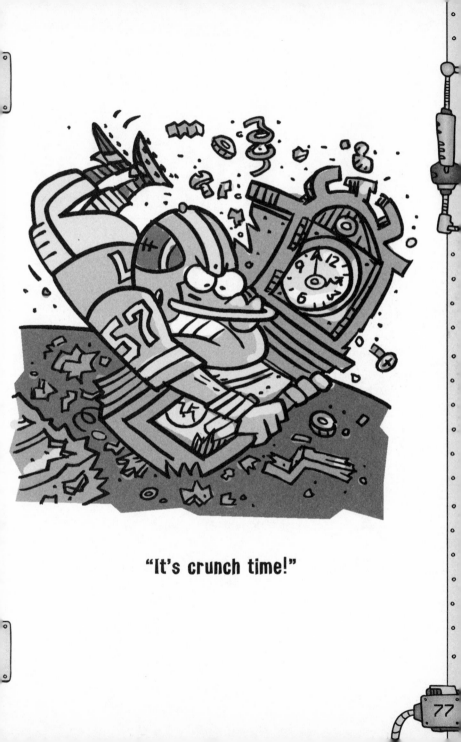

"It's crunch time!"

FLippin' OUT!

Strike Three?

1. Grab the bottom-right corner of page 79.

2. Flip page 79 back and forth without letting go.

3. Keep an eye on page 81.

4. If you flip fast enough, pages 79 and 81 will look like one, animated picture!

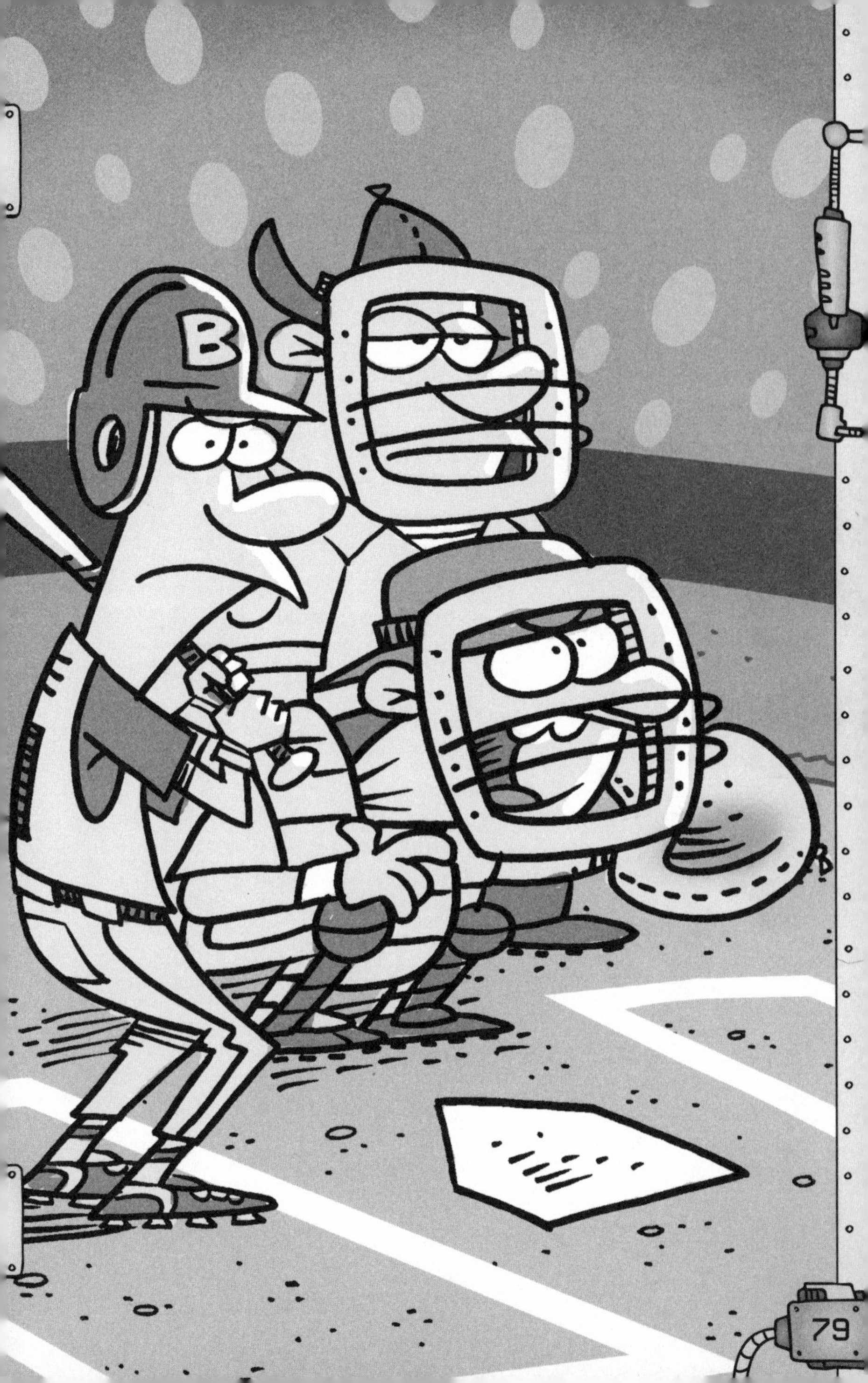
B

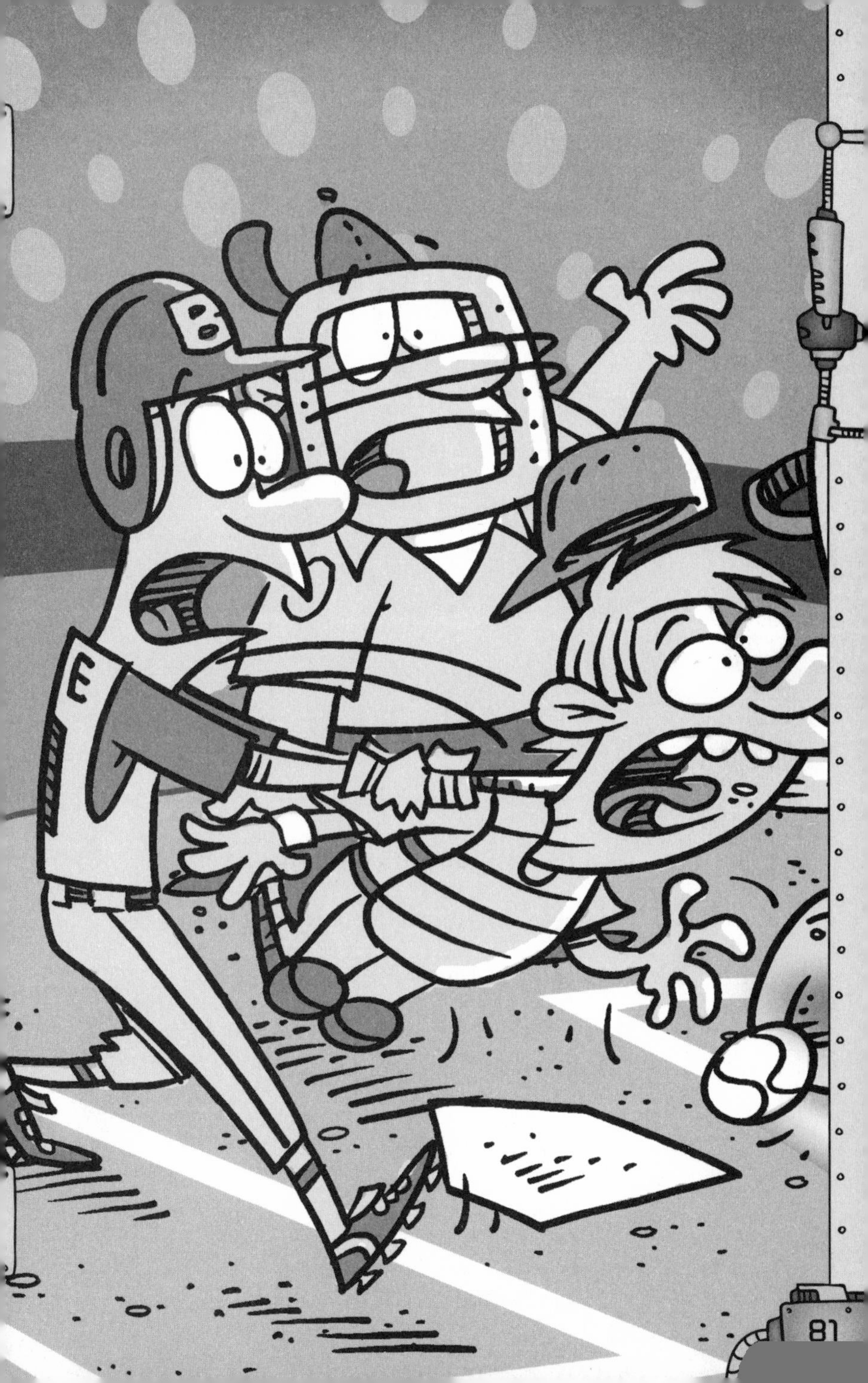
B
E

FLippin' OUT!

Spiked!

1. Grab the bottom-right corner of page 83.

2. Flip page 83 back and forth without letting go.

3. Keep an eye on page 85.

4. If you flip fast enough, pages 83 and 85 will look like one, animated picture!

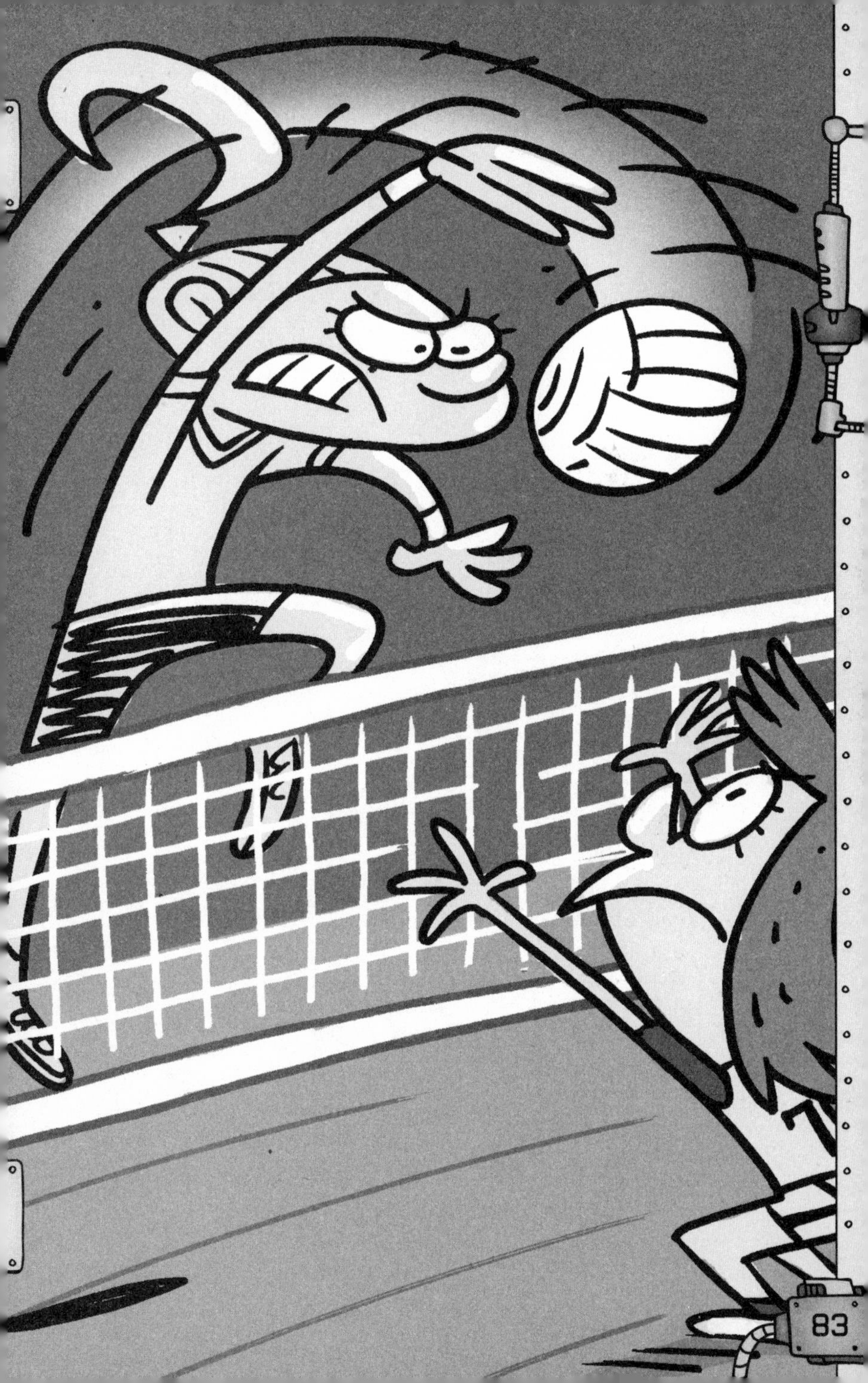

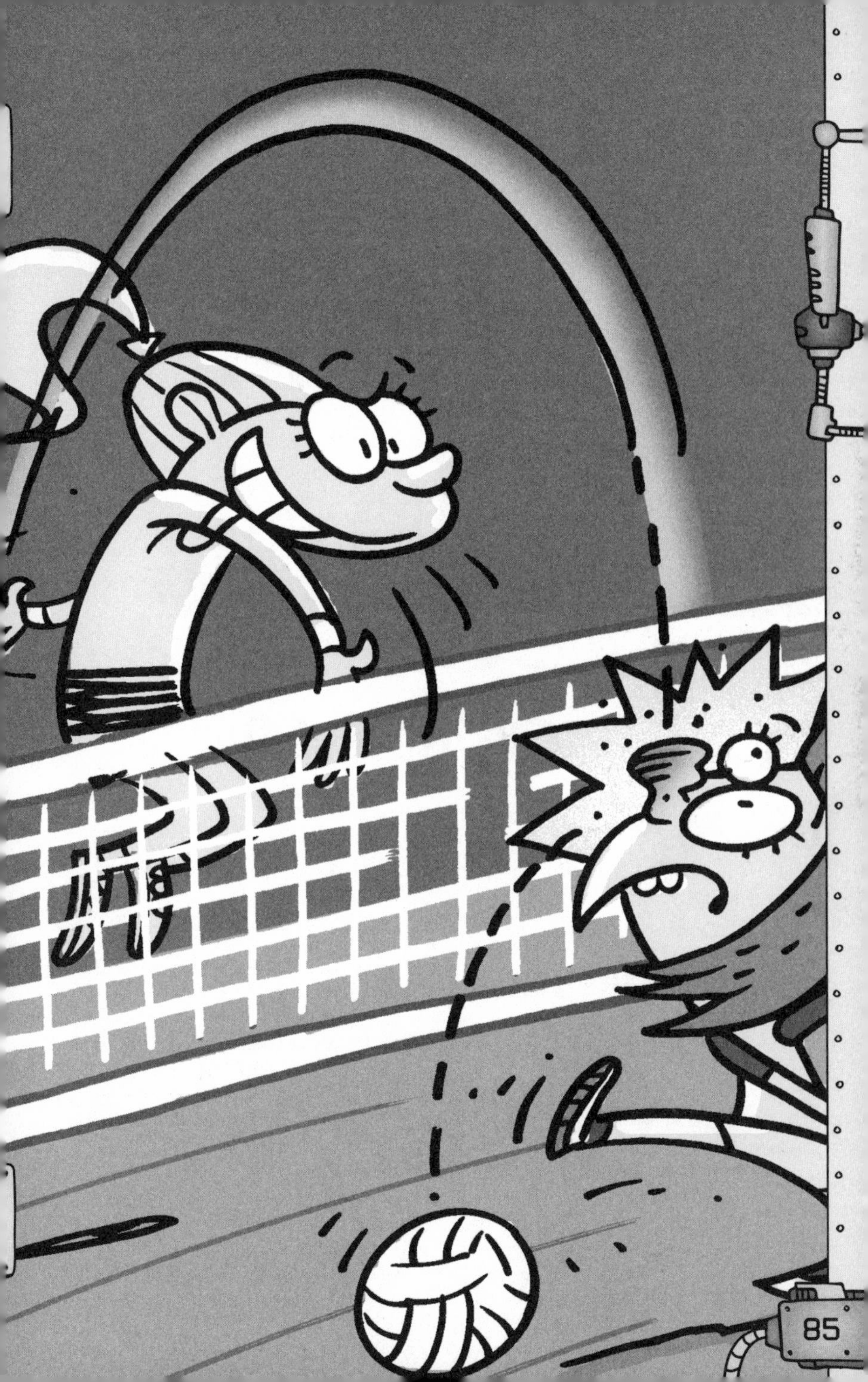

FLippin' OUT!

Touchdown Get Down!

1. Grab the bottom-right corner of page 87.

2. Flip page 87 back and forth without letting go.

3. Keep an eye on page 89.

4. If you flip fast enough, pages 87 and 89 will look like one, animated picture!

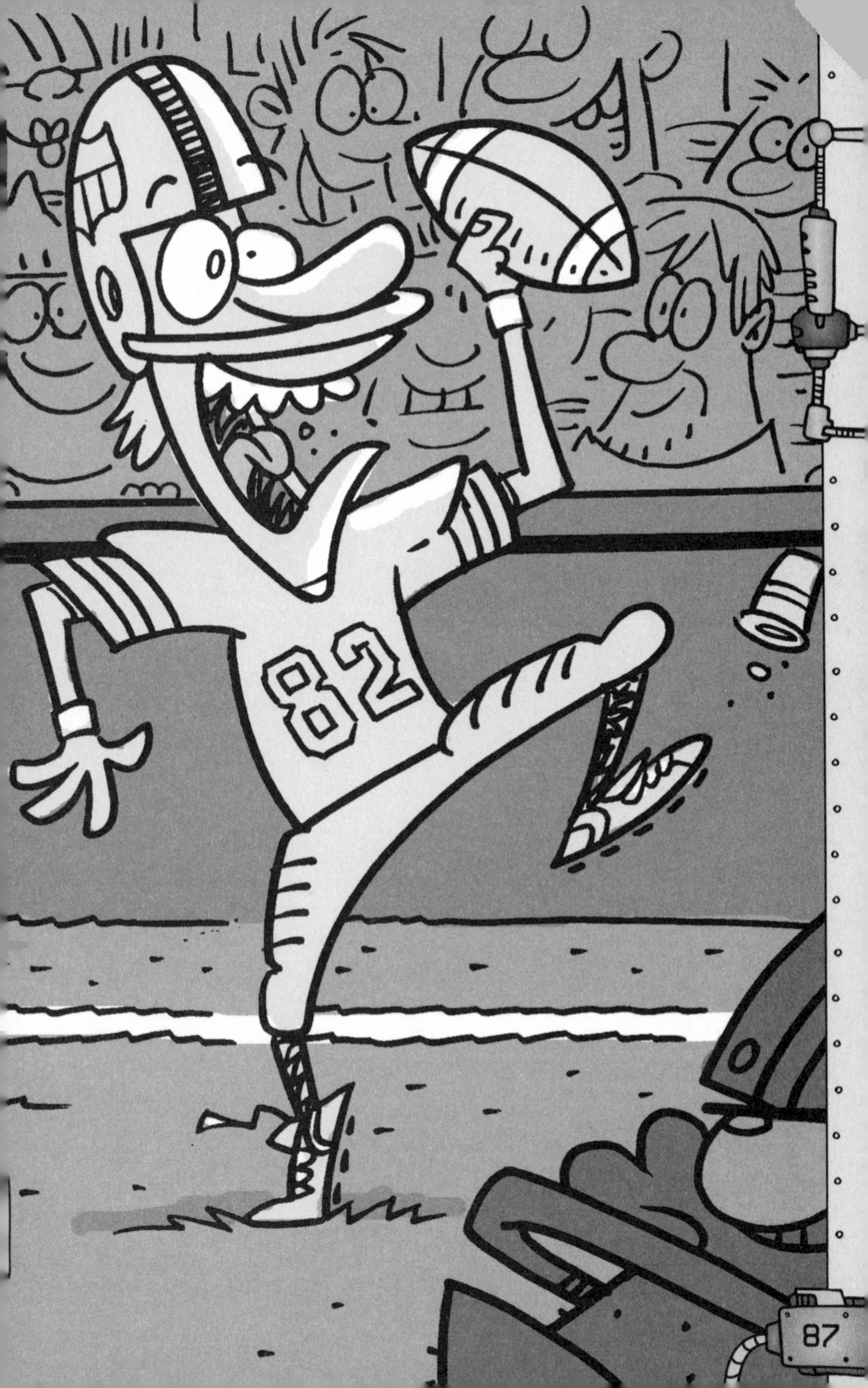
82

88

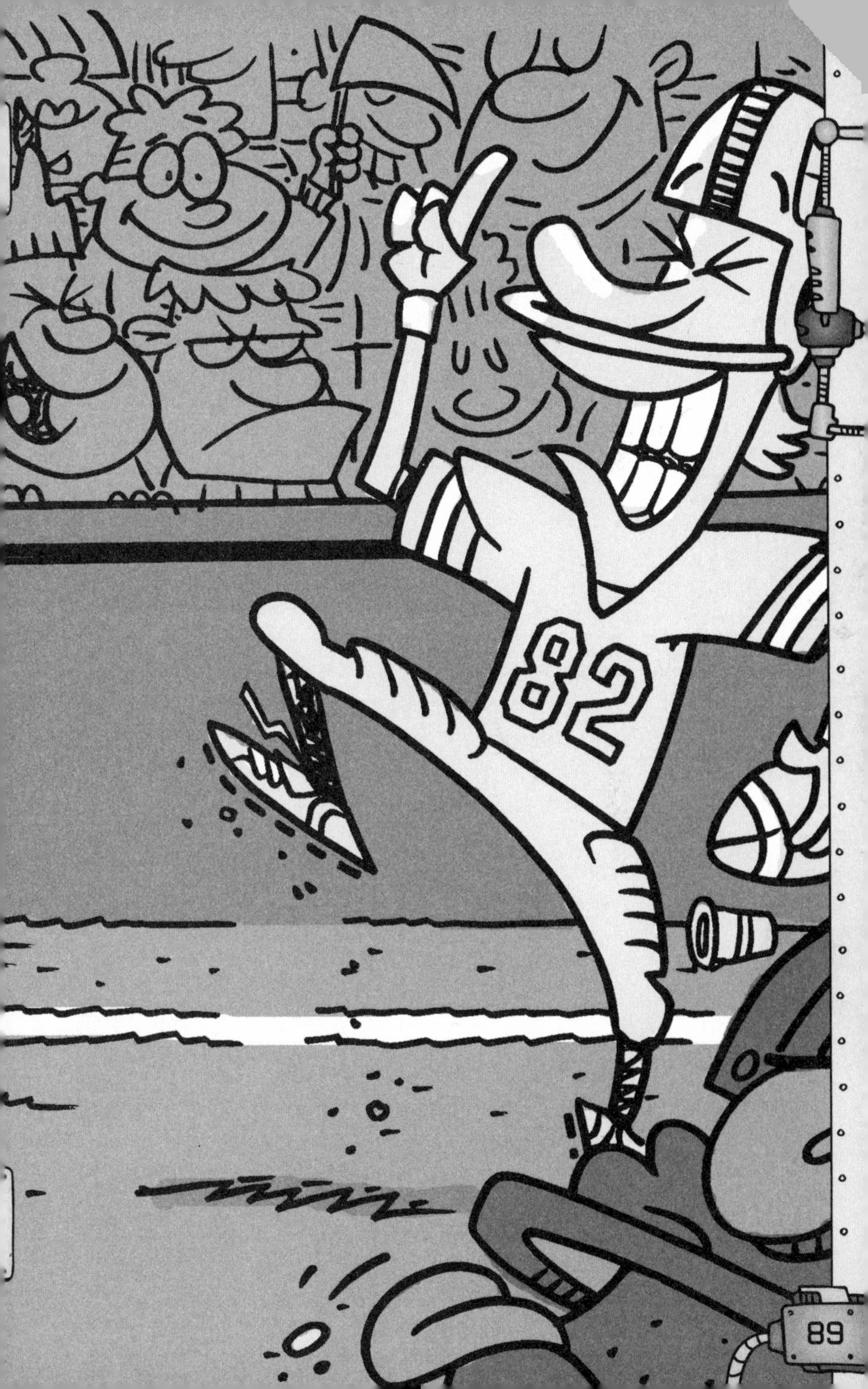
82

How to Draw
A FOOTBALL HELMET!

(YOU'LL NEED A PENCIL, A PIECE OF PAPER, AND AN ERASER.)

1. USING YOUR PENCIL, DRAW THE FIRST PART OF YOUR FOOTBALL HELMET, AS SHOWN BELOW.

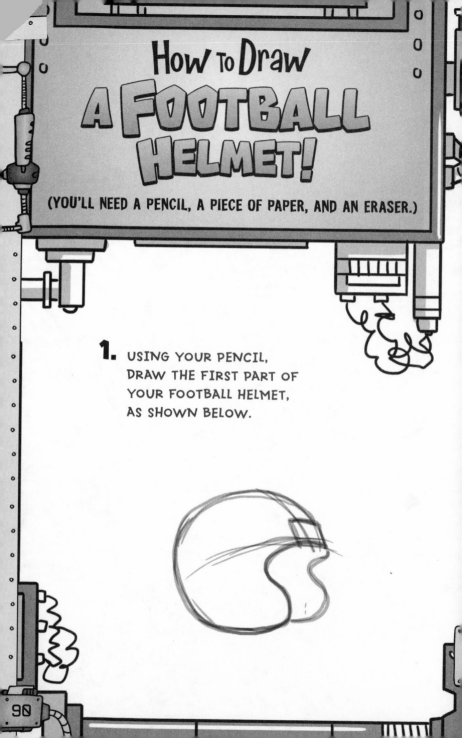

2. ADD A FACE MASK TO YOUR HELMET!

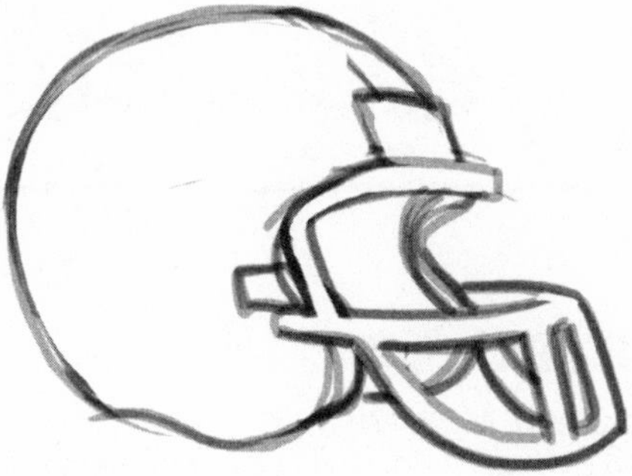

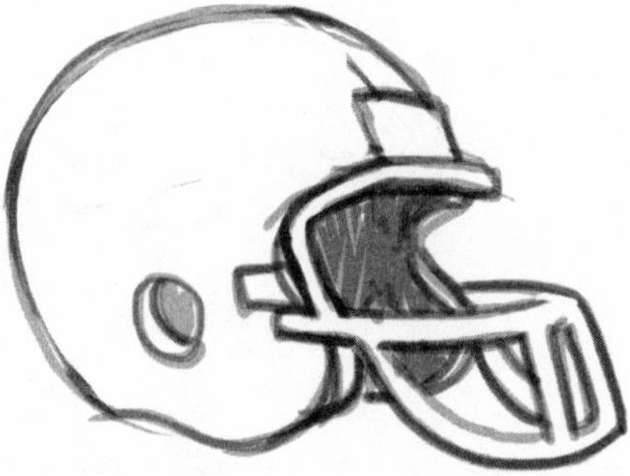

3. NEXT, SHADE THE INSIDE OF THE FOOTBALL HELMET WITH THE EDGE OF YOUR PENCIL.

4. FINALLY, ADD THE DETAILS AND THE LOGO OF YOUR FAVORITE SPORTS TEAM!

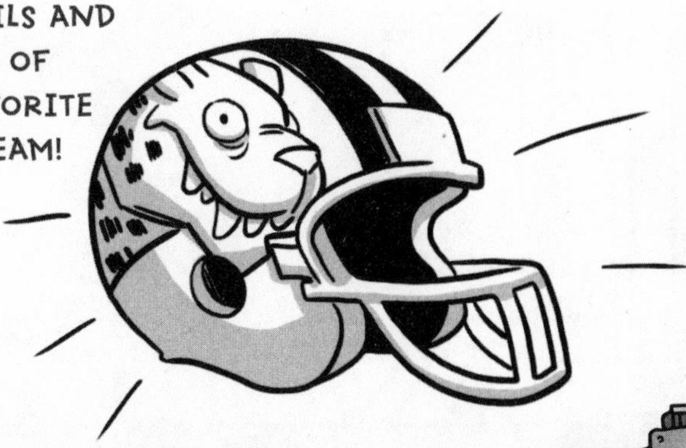

AUTHOR

MICHAEL DAHL

HAS WRITTEN MORE THAN 200 BOOKS FOR YOUNG READERS. HE IS THE AUTHOR OF THE SUPER-FUNNY JOKE BOOKS SERIES, *THE EVERYTHING KIDS' JOKE BOOKS,* THE SCINTILLATING *DUCK GOES POTTY,* AND TWO HUMOROUS MYSTERY SERIES: FINNEGAN ZWAKE (A "WISECRACKING RIOT" ACCORDING TO THE *CHICAGO TRIBUNE)* AND HOCUS POCUS HOTEL. HE TOURED THE COUNTRY WITH AN IMPROV TROUPE. AND BEGAN HIS AUSPICIOUS COMIC CAREER IN 5TH GRADE WHEN HIS STAND-UP ROUTINE MADE HIS MUSIC TEACHER LAUGH SO HARD SHE FELL OFF HER CHAIR. SHE IS NOT AVAILABLE FOR COMMENT.

ILLUSTRATORS

DOUGLAS HOLGATE

IS A FREELANCE ILLUSTRATOR, COMIC BOOK ARTIST, AND CARTOONIST BASED IN MELBOURNE, AUSTRALIA. HIS WORK HAS BEEN PUBLISHED ALL AROUND THE WORLD BY RANDOM HOUSE, SIMON AND SCHUSTER, THE NEW YORKER MAGAZINE, MAD MAGAZINE, IMAGE COMICS, AND MANY OTHERS. HIS WORKS FOR CHILDREN INCLUDE THE ZINC ALLOY AND BIKE RIDER SERIES (CAPSTONE), SUPER CHICKEN NUGGET BOY (HYPERION), AND A NEW SERIES OF POPULAR SCIENCE BOOKS BY DR. KARL KRUSZELNICKI (PAN MACMILLAN). DOUGLAS HAS SPORTED A POWERFUL, MANLY BEARD SINCE AGE 12 (PROBABLY NOT TRUE) AND IS ALSO A PRETTY RAD DUDE (PROBABLY TRUE).

DARYLL COLLINS

IS A FREELANCE CARTOONIST WHOSE WORK HAS APPEARED IN BOOKS, MAGAZINES, COMIC STRIPS, ADVERTISING, GREETING CARDS, PRODUCT PACKAGING AND CHARACTER DESIGN. HE ENJOYS MUSIC, MOVIES, BASEBALL, FOOTBALL, COFFEE, PIZZA, PETS, AND OF COURSE... CARTOONS!

More LAFF-O-TRONIC FUN!

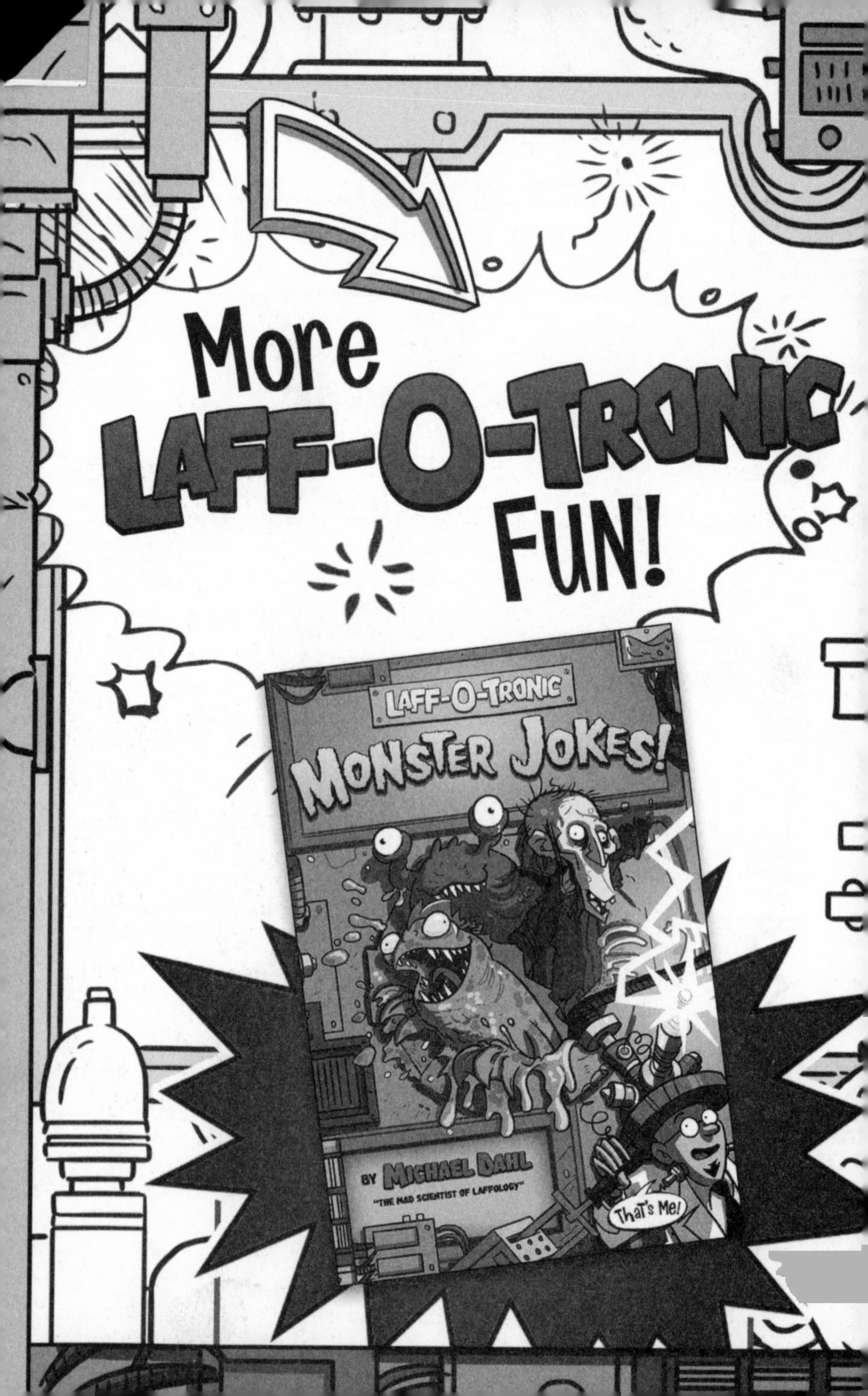
LAFF-O-TRONIC
MONSTER JOKES!
BY MICHAEL DAHL
"THE MAD SCIENTIST OF LAFFOLOGY"
That's Me!

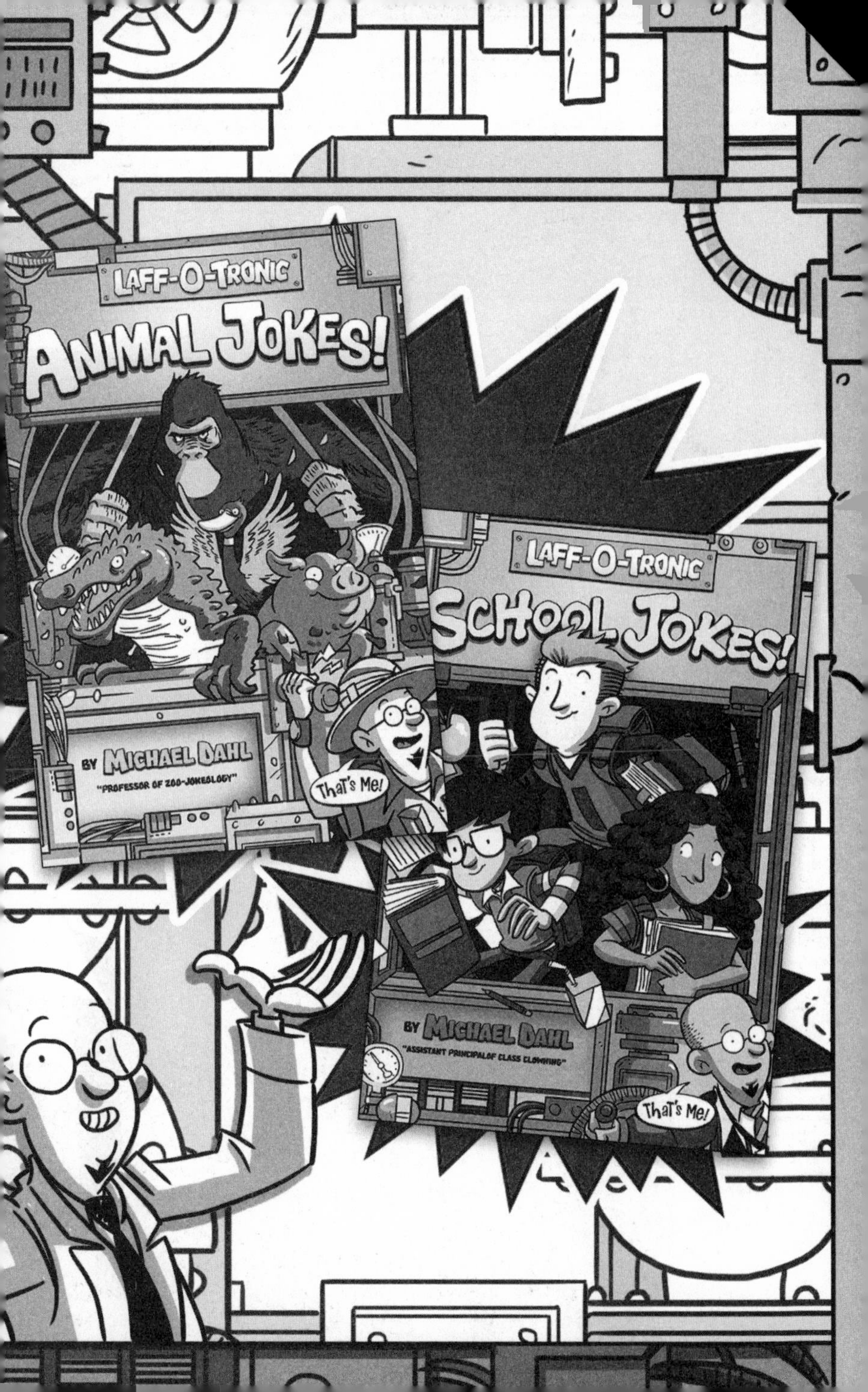
LAFF-O-TRONIC
ANIMAL JOKES!
BY MICHAEL DAHL
"PROFESSOR OF ZOO-JOKEOLOGY"
That's Me!
LAFF-O-TRONIC
SCHOOL JOKES!
BY MICHAEL DAHL
"ASSISTANT PRINCIPALOF CLASS CLOWNING"
That's Me!